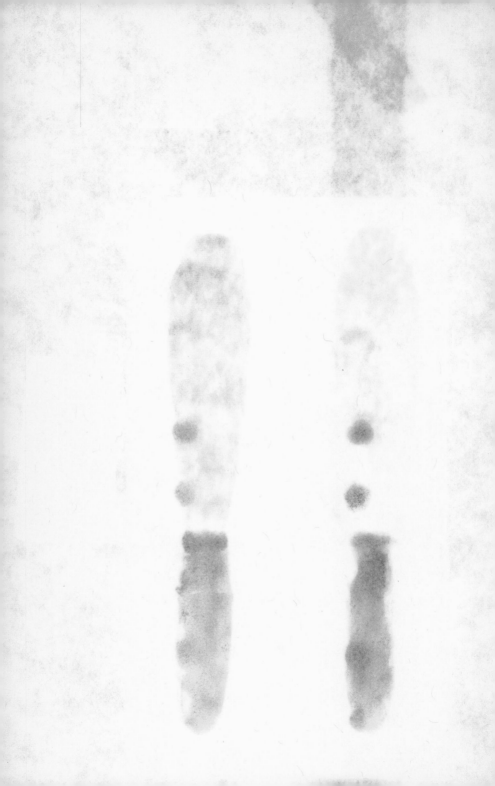

Cliff's Edge and Other Stories

Masaaki Tachihara

CLIFF'S EDGE
AND OTHER STORIES
Translated by Stephen W. Kohl

Cliff's Edge	薪	流	剣
The Archer		鏑	ヶ
Torchlight Nō	能	馬	崎

Ann Arbor, Michigan

Midwest Publishers, International

1980

Edited by Clark Malcolm

First Edition, First Printing, April, 1980

This book is distributed in Japan, Hong Kong, and South Korea by Western Publication Distribution Agency, Inc., 14-9 Okubo 3-chome, Shinjuku-ku, Tokyo, 160, Japan.

LIBRARY OF CONGRESS
CATALOG CARD NO.: 79-92855

    Tachihara, Masaaki, 1926 -
      Cliff's edge and other stories. Translated from the
    Japanese by Stephen W. Kohl.

        xvi, 193 p., 22 cm.

    Ann Arbor, Mich.: Midwest Publishers, International

    8003   791204

ISBN   0-936208-00-7

CONTENTS

Publisher's Note. ix

Translator's Note. xi

Introduction. xiii

Cliff's Edge 1

The Archer 89

Torchlight Nō. 125

Glossary. 193

PUBLISHER'S NOTE

The deaths of three great Japanese writers, Yasunari Kawabata, Juni-chiro Tanizaki, and Yukio Mishima, have left Japanese literature without a living and important representative in the West. It is my belief that Masaaki Tachihara will fill that void. The first translation of Mr. Tachihara's fiction into English, then, is a significant project — personally significant because my great-grandfather, Yoshibei Uchida, founded his publishing company in Tokyo one hundred years ago. Many deserve thanks for their help in it. First thanks go to Steve Kohl, whose skill and perception are the backbone of this volume. Many thanks, also, to my editor, Mr. Clark Malcolm, whose knowledge and diplomacy have gotten us and the stories over many rough passages. Mr. Katsuhiko Takeda, of Waseda University, and his advice have been invaluable. Professor Alan Howes and Andrew Mlynachik have spent long hours contributing toward my goal, and have been a great help. Professor Susumu Nagara, Professor Kathryn Sparling, Mr. Shunichi Katō, and Choowon Suh have also been valuable in various stages of the preparation of this volume. The author, to my great delight, has taken an active interest in this edition of his work, and it is my hope that these translations will give Mr. Tachihara the well-deserved respect of English-speaking readers.

Hitoshi Uchida
Publisher

TRANSLATOR'S NOTE

I would like to take this place to thank all those who assisted me in making these translations. In the first place, I am obligated to the University of Oregon Graduate School for the summer research award that enabled me to lay the groundwork for these translations. Considerable thanks, too, go to Shoji Kumagai and to Masako Aikawa who read the drafts of "Tsurugigasaki" and "Yabusame," respectively, and gave me many useful suggestions. I must also thank Ruth Bowman for reading a draft of "Takigi Nō" at a time when she surely had many other things to do. Finally, my gratitude goes to Sumiko Tazaki, who read and commented in detail on the versions of the first two stories, and whose encouragement helped me to undertake this project in the first place.

Stephen Kohl
Eugene, Oregon

INTRODUCTION

Tachihara Masaaki was born on January 6, 1926, in Taegu, Korea. His father was then a priest of the Zen sect teaching the history of Korean Buddhism and Zen at Hōteiji, a temple established more than a thousand years ago. At the age of four, Tachihara was sent to this temple to learn Chinese and Buddhist scriptures from the elderly scholar-priest, Muyō Shōkei. It was there, through observing the lives of the priests, that Tachihara became conscious of the idea that human beings must be totally self-reliant.

Tachihara's writings often include the sentence, "Although winter may have passed, there is no assurance that spring will come." This, too, Tachihara learned from Zen. He constantly reminds himself and us of the harshness of human life and that it is our fate to bear this harshness.

When Tachihara was six years old, his father committed suicide. While there was no publicly announced explanation, the fact that he was of mixed Japanese-Korean blood must not be overlooked. Tachihara's father belonged to the aristocratic Korean house of Yi, while his grandmother was Japanese. With the annexation of Korea by Japan, members of the intelligentsia like Tachihara's father were forced to question their new position and their own identities. After studying Buddhism at a university in Kyoto, Tachihara's father was commissioned as an officer in the Japanese army. His reasons for leaving the army and becoming a priest are uncertain, but it is clear that he suffered over questions about how men should conduct their lives.

The suicide had a decisive influence on Tachihara's life. Walter H. Pater, in "The Child in the House," writes of the shocking impact of his own father's death. That death left an indelible mark that appears as the contemplation of death in Pater's writing. In a similar way, Tachihara's father's suicide remains with Tachihara always.

After the suicide, the Tachihara family moved to Andong, and Tachihara was enrolled in an elementary school for Japanese children. But because of his mixed blood, he was constantly taunted by his classmates, and finally he injured one of them. He was then placed in a school for Korean children, but he could not escape being tormented by the problem of identity. His mother, too, was of mixed Japanese-Korean parentage. Her father was Japanese, and her mother, a member of the Yi family. Tachihara was to be doubly haunted by the problem.

Tachihara's mother's family was Catholic. As in "Jesus and Judas," another of Tachihara's stories, this part of Tachihara's background surfaces in his work. The conflicting beliefs of Catholicism and Buddhism also left their mark on Tachihara.

Tachihara's mother remarried in 1935 and left for Japan, taking Tachihara's younger brother with her. Tachihara was sent to Taegu to live with a physician uncle. There he learned to play the piano and even took lessons in traditional Korean pottery. It was a lonely life, but it was a time when there were many opportunities to be exposed to art and beauty. Tachihara was still very young when he learned to appreciate beauty and to create beauty for himself. Even though he was forced to part with his parents at an early age, wealth provided him with a good education and constant exposure to the arts—circumstances which make it possible for him to create beauty in the present.

When Tachihara first arrived in Japan in December of 1937, he went to live with his mother's elder sister in Yokosuka. Again the problem of his mixed blood arose, and his school life was far from pleasant. In high school he was involved in another incident in which another person was injured. He had begun earlier to practice *kendo*, the Japanese martial art similar to fencing, and was already training himself to the life of a model Japanese warrior, a life demanding excellence in both military and literary skills.

Two years before the Japanese defeat, Tachihara enrolled in Keijo (Soeul) Imperial University, and this provided an opportunity to visit Andong and Taegu and to reminisce. Weak lungs, however, forced him to terminate his studies in Korea and to return to one of his mother's relative's homes in Kamakura. Kamakura has been the home of many Japanese writers, including Kawabata and Yasunari, and unlike today was then a quiet town of many ancient temples. There Tachihara came into contact with traditional Japan and became determined to make literature his life.

After the war, Tachihara began studying at Waseda University, concentrating on medieval Japanese literature and especially the medieval dramatist Zeami, scholar and theorist of the Nō. These studies were to have a great deal of influence on his work.

Tachihara began publishing his short stories in 1956, and in 1960, the first story in this collection, "Cliff's Edge," was nominated for the Akutagawa Prize, the most coveted of the awards for young writers. Another story was later nominated for the same prize, but for reasons which are not clear, Tachihara was awarded the Naoki Prize instead for the story "White Poppies" in 1961. While the Naoki Prize is also highly regarded, it is usually given to works that have wide popular appeal. Naoki Prize winners, consequently, have the tendency to be labelled "popular" writers by the reading public. It is regrettable for both Tachihara and Japanese literature that he has been so categorized and his work so classified.

"Cliff's Edge" is a short story concerned with the problem of identity faced by a youth of mixed blood and set against the background of the Japanese defeat in World War II and the subsequent independence of Korea. The motif is, of course, taken directly from Tachihara's own experiences with war and the problems of mixed blood. Kenkichi opposes Tarō's marriage to Shizuko, not because the two lovers are cousins, but because of Tarō's Japanese and Korean background. Although the fact may be otherwise, Japanese tend to believe in the "purity" of their race, and therefore, the problem of mixed blood is much more complicated than it is in the United States. Since persons of mixed blood are a tiny minority, they are forced to endure a great deal of unreasonable persecution and are burdened with all kinds of social handicaps. Tachihara portrays the miserable existence of Jirō, Yasumasa, and Kyŏng-hyo Yi, who come very close to grasping the reasons for their suffering and to dealing with it. That they are able to transcend this world is the most important lesson Tachihara learned from Zen.

Masako, the protagonist of "The Archer," is a woman with large reserves of emotional strength. "It is by suicide that Masako can simultaneously get revenge on her husband and prove her fidelity to Takeji." Her strong personality reminds one of Makiko Kito in Mishima's *Runaway Horses*. Of course, Masako is by nature more innocent than Makiko, and yet her strength of will allows her to choose death as a meaningful way to assert her position. At the moment of death, Masako finds perfected beauty in "the quick snap of the arrow being released, the long hum of the arrow cutting through the air, the short smack as it hit the target." To Tachihara, supreme beauty is created in death.

The final story in this collection, "Torchlight Nō," resembles "The Archer" in its depiction of beauty in death. The protagonist, Masako, is drawn to her cousin Shuntarō, because of her husband's unfaithfulness. The psychological change in Masako is given in detail and with stark realism. In addition, the experience of the beauty of the Nō and the lovers' double suicide are more minutely described than in "The Archer."

In all three stories, love between close relatives is an important element. Assuming that love between cousins is somehow inevitable, Tachihara uses the theme to show human beings so driven that they cannot accept their fates and so tormented that they must deal with who and what they really are. The characters are made to bear a variety of much more severe consequences than those entailed in an ordinary illicit love. These themes arise directly from Tachihara's own experience. For someone of mixed blood, the problem is not merely one of personal freedom. Tachihara's characters come to comprehend this—a comprehension often leading to death. Tachihara pursues human psychology to its limits, and it is this that makes his works significant contributions to contemporary literature.

Katz Takeda
Professor of Comparative Literature
Waseda University
Tokyo, Japan

Editor's note: The McCune-Reischauer system of romanization was used in this volume for the Korean names.

An asterisk indicates an entry in the glossary.

CLIFF'S EDGE

1

When Yasumasa had finished reading the letter, he returned it to Jirō and stared out the window. Then he began the formal ritual of preparing tea. Jirō watched his grandfather manipulate the tea whisk and thought, 'This letter must have surprised even grandfather.' Jirō looked outside. It was a summer morning and the mountain was alive with the incessant cries of cicadas. Cicadas were even humming on the bamboo fence in the style of the Kenninji Temple that surrounded the Nō pavilion where they sat. Faces of people who had died or departed, faces of people as they had been at a certain moment on a certain day, flashed in Jirō's mind. These faces were dyed with the color of the various seasons he associated with each person.

The air mail letter had arrived shortly after Jirō's wife had taken the two children and gone down the mountain to go shopping. It had been postmarked in Seoul, Korea. Jirō gasped and felt dizzy for a moment when he saw the name Kyŏng-hyo Yi. Yi had been a Captain in the Japanese Imperial Army and at the outbreak of the North China Incident had disappeared from his unit stationed at Taegu, Kyongsan Puckto. His whereabouts had never been traced. This was not just a letter from someone far away, it was a letter from someone Jirō had thought he would never hear from again. The letter itself was extremely plain: 'In mid-September, on my way to the United States, I will stop over in Japan and see you for the first time in twenty-five years. I have heard the story of Tarō's sudden death. I will only be staying in Japan for two days, but I expect there will be time to visit Tarō's grave.' That was all. Jirō began to unravel his childhood memories. He thought his father's uniformed figure could only be described as 'dignified.' For twenty-five years he had not shed a tear; he had watched dry-eyed as the world changed and now his mind returned to the past when some days had seemed to last a year. Still, he could not imagine what kind of life his father had led for those twenty-five years. The tone of the letter was casual, like something a father would send to his family while he was away on a trip. Jirō could not comprehend the feelings of this soldier named Kyŏng-hyo Yi. The landscape of his memory was completely dark. Jirō felt as though he had been trying to escape this darkness since the end of the War, that he was obsessed with fleeing it. He no longer felt involved in events. There was a long period when he felt as though his heart was no longer moved by things, when he had felt nothing.

Yasumasa put down the tea whisk and asked, "Shall I prepare tea for you?"

"No, that's fine. I don't care for tea when the weather is this hot."

"About your father—Five years ago I ran into a man who was at the military academy at the same time as your father, and I learned that he is now an important man in Korea, but somehow at the time I did not feel that I could tell you about that."

"I see—Grandfather, do you hate my father for abandoning his wife and children?"

"No. He was a fine man. My own feeling was that it is not necessary to pry into the past. You will succeed me as head of the Iwami family, and I wondered if I should tell you that your father had become a Korean citizen and that he is actually alive."

"Grandfather, even now that I know my father is still living, my feelings have not changed. I, too, have no intention of digging into the past. I just want to get away from those dark memories I have of the years we spent at Tsurugigasaki; that's all I want. I think you feel the same way, grandfather."

"Indeed, everything was dark and gloomy in those days. Jirō, I think it would be a good idea if you did not brood any more about not being pure Japanese. Even if you worry about it, there is nothing you can do. You would be happier studying literature, even if there is no money in it. Your father was a fine man, but I didn't understand him. He was my nephew, but he was also half Korean and in that sense he inhabited a world I knew nothing of. If your father had not been a soldier, I might have understood him better."

"What do you mean?"

"When your uncle Naoto brought you boys back to Japan, it occurred to me that your father had planned it that way all along. After all, hadn't he studied at the military academy? He was an outstanding soldier and it is a pity Japan lost him. Well, that's all in the past now. Judging from this letter, your father seems to have some idea of the things that have happened here. Let's greet him warmly when he comes — But how shall we tell him about Tarō's death?"

"I don't think that is something you have to worry about, grandfather. Father left us during the summer of the year I was eleven years old, and I have no idea what his life has been like since then, but I don't suppose the death of anyone here means much to my father. After all, he is the kind of person who could register his children as Japanese citizens and then abandon them along with his wife in order to go his own way. Grandfather, there is only a very little Korean blood flowing in my veins. I have been raised in Japan and I am studying the Japanese classics. I am a Japanese, and there is a difference between me and my father who is a Korean. Even though he is half Japanese, he is still a Korean, and that will not change even if I meet him."

"I am not worrying about it."

"Michiko will be returning any moment now. I think I will go out for a while."

"Are you going to Hisako's place?"

"No. There is no point in visiting mother. I thought I would go and visit the three graves at Tsurugigasaki. Since last year I have been brooding about what happened and I want to get rid of these gloomy memories. I will take the opportunity of father's visit to place some flowers on the graves."

"Yes, do that, that will make me happy. I must be getting old; all I can remember is the bitterness of it all."

"On the way back, I will stop at Misaki and buy some abalone."

When Jirō left the Nō pavilion, he went down to the main house through the humming intensity of the cicadas' incessant cries. Logs had been buried in the hillside to make nine steps leading into the garden where the main house stood bleached by the wind and rains of forty years and even the white plaster walls were dingy. Since he had continued with his leisurely researches as a literary scholar, he did not have the means of reviving the declining fortunes of the Iwami family, and eventually he would have to sell this old family home and move with his grandfather into a smaller house. His grandfather, Yasumasa, had anticipated this turn of events and did not utter a word of complaint, but spent his days shut up in the Nō pavilion reading his old books. The old man enjoyed making tea for his friends who came occasionally to sing Nō chants. After Jirō had returned to the house and changed into Western clothes, he went down the mountain.

Tsurugigasaki. It is a promontory thrust out like the tip of a sword from the Miura Peninsula in the Southeast part of Kanagawa Prefecture. It is situated directly across from Sunosaki in Chiba Prefecture; these two points form the entrance to Tokyo Bay. There is a lighthouse on the tip of this promontory. The people who live in the area call it Kensaki rather than Tsurugigasaki.

Jirō bought some chrysanthemums in the town of Kurihama and then got on the regular bus to Tsurugigasaki.

By the time it had crossed Nobi Pass and was going through Kita Shimoura, he could see Tsurugigasaki in front of them and off to the left, stabbing far out into the sea. Seventeen years ago when he had gone out in a fishing boat to search for Shizuko's body he had seen Tsurugigasaki from the sea. He was nineteen years old that summer and felt as though he had caught a glimpse of his own death in those white cliffs, but now Tsurugigasaki was lying on its side unchanged, shrouded in the light of late August.

The surrounding landscape had not changed a bit in seventeen years. Some sixteen years ago he had moved to Kamakura, but the image of Tsurugigasaki he had retained in his mind was the way it had looked in the summer of 1945.

As the bus passed Matsuwa, the lighthouse came into view. He felt emotion gently welling up in his breast as he recalled a winter day he had walked along this road with his brother.

Presently the bus reached the end of the line. He got off on a steep road that cut through the hills choked with silverberry. On the right was a sharp, deep valley. The lighthouse was situated beside the valley on a promontory that thrust out into the sea. He made his way past the house he had once lived in and went to the graves in the pine grove on the left. When he had sold the property, he retained this one flat corner with its three graves that were now overgrown with summer grass. All around were clusters of asters and silverberry. Placing his offering of chrysanthemums before the graves, he clasped his hands in prayer.

What had his brother or Shizuko protected or accomplished in exchange for their lives? Navy Commander Kyŏng-myŏng Yi who had committed suicide here at the end of the War, would be remembered neither in Japanese history nor in Korean history. Thoughts of these three people welled up in Jirō's mind like an endless spring. After a while he left the grove. The house he had once lived in seemed empty and desolate.

Presently he came to the entrance of the lighthouse. The stone-paved road was lined on both sides with black pines bent over sharply by the sea winds. It was just as it had always been. He went up the road. The slope falling away to the valley on the right was overgrown with summer grasses and the lighthouse glittered in the brilliant August sunlight. He went past the cluster of lighthouse buildings and came out on top of the cliffs on the tip of the headland. There before him, but separated by a chasm, were two stone outcroppings about as high as where he stood. When the tide was out, there was a strip of stony shingle where a number of women gathered seaweed, and beyond, at the very edge of the shingle, were men fishing. The Bōsō Peninsula across the bay was hazy and one could barely make out the shape of Mt. Nokogiri.

He sat down on the grass and gazed out over the vast reaches of Sagami Bay on one side and at the Bōsō Peninsula on the other. He had never gotten around to asking his grandfather why he had built his retreat on this desolate stretch of seacoast and now that the house had passed into other hands, he felt no urge to raise the question.

From the autumn of 1937 through the spring of 1946 he had lived here on the tip of the sword, so to speak. This was the first time he had come back to visit Tsurugigasaki which had, in a sense, been his companion during those years. Was there really any significance in the fact that he had not come back to visit the place? He had been abandoned by his father, left behind by his mother, his brother had died. Was it because the sadness of all this had some hold over his heart? But that was only the superficial reason. His feelings about Tsurugigasaki were related to the fact that he had consciously examined the chaotic mixture of blood in the dark recesses of his mind. Now as he sat on top of the cliffs, bathed in August sunlight, he thought back over the various shapes Tsurugigasaki had had during those eight years. He felt the murmur of the sea and the whisper of the salt wind within him. Tsurugigasaki, symbolized by the white lighthouse, remained in his memory, Tsurugigasaki of the white cliffs. Tsurugigasaki as it had appeared one year wrapped in spring sunlight, presented an image of infinite kindness. Another time, in winter, Tsurugigasaki thrust its fangs out into the wind-whipped waves and transformed itself into a demon about to consume him. There were yet other seasons when he could not see Tsurugigasaki taking these forms. Tsurugigasaki presented such images when he saw it from unexpected perspectives, and there were times when it caused him to lose his bearings. Tsurugigasaki had destroyed his brother, devoured his cousin, had caused his uncle to commit suicide. 'What does Tsurugigasaki mean to me?' His thoughts went back to the time before he had lived here.

In the summer of 1937 the family was living in Taegu, Korea. Jirō was in the fifth grade, his brother Tarō was in the first year of middle school. In July that year the North China Incident occured and the two boys could not enjoy a typical summer vacation. They were taken to Taegu Station every day to see off the soldiers who were leaving for the north. The boys' home was located on the estate of their paternal grandmother in Meiji-chō. Their father, Kyŏng-hyo Yi commuted from there to his unit, the Taegu Regiment.

One evening in early August the boys' father returned home from his unit, changed from his uniform into civilian clothes, and went out without waiting for dinner. He never came back. The next day an officer from the same outfit came and asked their mother Hisako a few questions and left. The following morning three members of the military police appeared and searched the home. They confiscated several books and a photograph taken of Yi at the military academy. On the third day, Hisako was summoned to regimental headquarters and was taken there by the military police. She seemed exhausted when she returned that evening. After that, from time to time the boys saw their mother weeping quietly as though remembering the past. Their father never returned.

September came and with it the beginning of the new school term, but the brothers were not allowed to go out. Finally, their Uncle Naoto came from Japan and took the mother and children back to Kamakura to their maternal grandfather's house. A plainclothesman escorted the family all the way to Kamakura, and even after they arrived, a policeman would show up at the house every day and ask the same question each time, "Have you received any messages from Kyŏng-hyo Yi?" After staying a month at the grandfather's house, the family was forced to move to Tsurugigasaki. At this point the brothers really understood what was happening. For a long time afterwards Jirō carried with him the memory of the strange feeling he had had when the secret police showed up at their house in Taegu.

The plainclothesman even accompanied them to Tsurugigasaki. Their mother was restricted in her movements and whenever she wanted to leave the vicinity of Tsurugigasaki had to make a request in advance at the police box nearby. Tarō enrolled in the Yokosuka Middle School and Jirō in the Tsurugigasaki Elementary School. Hisako spent her days gazing at the lighthouse and the waters of Sagami Bay. Naturally, the boys gazed at the lighthouse, too. Gradually, before the eyes of the mother and her children, Tsurugigasaki began to transform itself.

Jirō never learned how it leaked out, but during his third week at school he was questioned by one of his new classmates, "You're not pure Japanese, are you?" Then a few days later the rumor began to spread. "He's a Korean, his dad's a Red."

"Is it true?" a fisherman's son asked him.

"Well, my mother is Japanese and my father's mother is Japanese too," replied Jirō uneasily.

"You talk funny. Can't you say, 'me' or 'dad' or 'my old lady'? Even if your mom is Japanese, you aren't really Japanese. That's for sure." The fisherman's son gave him a mean look. Some of the village families were farmers; the rest were fishermen, and many of his classmates were the children of fishermen.

Thus it was that the two years Jirō spent at the Tsurugigasaki Elementary School were shadowed with dark memories. The sea was just across the street in front of the school; it was a shallow, sharply curved inlet studded with seaweed weirs. One of his classmates took seaweed from the weirs and shared it with Jirō. Enjoying the delicate flavor of fresh seaweed or catching fish with his bare hands in the deep tidal pools when the tide was out were the only pleasant memories he had.

Eventually Jirō finished his studies at Tsurugigasaki Elementary School and went on to the Yokosuka Middle School. Since Yokosuka was a large Navy base, many of the students at the new school were the children of military parents and it produced a large number of graduates who enrolled in the Army and Navy academies each year. Tarō was a third year student the year Jirō entered the school. It was unusual for students in their third year to begin studying for their college entrance examinations. The place had a strong military flavor since most of the students had their sights set on the military academies, and even if they had some physical defect such as poor eyesight, they would be aiming at the Quartermaster's School. In the midst of all this, Tarō led a life different from any of the other students. It was his hope to enter the Science Department at the Third Higher School in Kyoto, but he did not study for his examinations, and spent his time after classes in the auditorium playing the piano.

"Don't you care whether or not you pass the entrance examination this year?" asked his brother. It was the spring of 1940 and they were returning home after the opening ceremonies for the new school term. That was the year Jirō was in the second year of middle school.

"No. I will definitely go to Kyoto next spring. Are you worried I won't make it?" asked Tarō rather defensively.

"You probably have complete confidence, but—"

"You really want to ask why I don't try to get into the Literature Department."

"That's right."

"It's a matter of expedience, quite simply a matter of not wanting to get drafted. It is stupid to go out and get hit by a bullet and die in a ditch somewhere. When Uncle Kyŏng-myŏng was here the other day, he said the war would go on for years. I figure that if I spend three years at the higher school and three years at Kyoto University, and then stay on for some graduate work, the war should be over."

Jirō's thoughts turned to his uncle, Kyŏng-myŏng Yi, to whom he had said farewell some two weeks ago. Kyŏng-myŏng, a Navy Commander, had been working in the Yokosuka Navy Yards, but was transferred to Maizuru on the Japan Sea Coast. "I won't be seeing you for a while," he said. Kyŏng-myŏng did not know anything about his brother, Kyŏng-hyo. In response to Hisako's question he had said that obviously Kyŏng-hyo was neither in Japan nor Korea. His desertion from the army had put their father, Kyŏng-yun Yi, in a difficult position, and it also handicapped his younger brothers who were living in Tokyo. Still, their well-being was assured by the treaty of 1910. When Japan annexed Korea and brought the Yi Dynasty (1392-1910) to an end, provisions were made to insure the livelihood of the aristocratic families. Kyŏng-myŏng mentioned that he too was constantly under surveillance.

"Uncle Kyŏng-myŏng will have no choice but to stay in the Navy the rest of his life. Do you realize what that means?"

"Yes."

"The Korean Imperial family and aristocrats were provided with Japanese girls and they tried to produce mixed blooded children. It was ridiculous."

In order to return home, Jirō walked to Ōtsu Station where he got on the Keihin express to Uraga. From there he took the bus to Misaki and got off at Matsuwa. The trip took about two and a half hours each way. During the summer he rode his bicycle to school except when it was raining, but in winter he used public transportation.

That day as the brothers got off the bus at Matsuwa, they met Aoki, the son of a fisherman who attended the Yokosuka Private Middle School. Aoki stopped his bicycle and asked Jirō, "Going home?"

"Yeah. Where are you going?"

"I have some business at the City Hall in Minami Shimoura," Aoki went on his way.

"Who was that?" asked Tarō.

"That's Aoki. He used to give me fresh seaweed very often."

"Is he a fisherman? I don't remember him."

"Why? Do you look down on fishermen?"

"I despise human beings. Especially soldiers."

"But our uncle is a soldier, isn't he, and as far as that goes, our father is a soldier too."

"What a pair of brothers they make. I just can't figure them out."

"You shouldn't talk that way."

"Why not? One became a Korean and deserted the army, and the other became a Japanese and pretends to be loyal to the Emperor. Grandfather himself is a Korean, but I can't imagine what he thought he was doing when he enrolled his two sons, one in the Army Academy and the other in the Navy Academy. Think about it. Is it really possible for one to become a Korean and the other to be a Japanese? Of course not. Mixed bloods can't be one or the other. They are like that mongrel dog that hangs around here."

"Do you keep thinking about this? Brooding about it all the time?"

"No. The only thing I brood about day and night is how to play the piano well."

On this occasion Jirō felt as though he had caught a glimpse of what was going on in his brother's mind.

"There's a Korean in your class, isn't there?" asked Jirō.

"You mean Yong-gyu Kim? He seems to think he's a friend of mine, but I always act like a Japanese in front of him. But, of course, in front of Japanese I make a point to act like a Korean. It irritates me when people think they can be friends with a person who is caught in the middle, who can become neither one nor the other. What about you? Isn't there a real, honest-to-goodness half-breed in your class?"

"There is one, but we stay away from each other."

"Both of you feel the same way, then?"

"I guess so."

"Isn't that rather strange? In terms of blood percentage, you are more Japanese than he is. Well, in either case there is not all that much difference. C'mon, let's hurry home, I'm hungry. We may not be able to eat mom's home cooking much longer."

"What do you mean by that?"

"Last time the old man came down from Kamakura, I heard him urging mother to remarry. He wants her to marry some friend of Uncle Naoto whose wife died recently. He lives in Odawara. After we eat, we can go fishing. The ocean croakers are just beginning to bite now."

Tarō began walking faster. Jirō lagged behind, hoping that what his brother said was not true.

2

The late August sunlight was strong on the top of the cliffs and he could not stay there for long. Getting to his feet, Jirō recalled that it was about a year later that Tsurugigasaki began to mean something very different to him. His thoughts turned to his brother who had finished the four years of middle school and qualified for the Third Higher School. Jirō remembered the spring day his brother left for Kyoto.

There was no bus at the bus stop when Jirō got there,

so he decided to walk to Matsuwa. From there he could get a bus to Misaki where he would buy abalone and return home. He wiped the sweat from his face as he walked.

Tarō carried out his plans, and having finished middle school, he qualified for the Third Higher School and left Tsurugigasaki at the beginning of April. Hisako's second marriage and departure for her new family occurred in May of that year. Earlier, at the beginning of January, their cousin Shizuko was brought to Tsurugigasaki from Kamakura by her grandparents. She had a lung ailment and required a change of air. Once a week her family doctor would come from Kamakura. Jirō, who was a year younger, considered the sixteen year old Shizuko to be a woman. She had a slender body, large eyes, and a beautiful, high voice. She spent her days in her room which was filled with the fragrance of incense. During the brief period between the time Shizuko came and Tarō left for Kyoto, Jirō knew of nothing that might have happened between them.

"If you leave me, I'll die!" One day at noon Jirō heard Shizuko make this anguished declaration. It was a warm day at the end of March. Jirō was just coming around the base of a large rock in search of his brother who was fishing at the edge of the stony beach. Although they were brothers, they were quite different and Jirō had never envied his brother's pale complexion more than he did now. Tarō and Shizuko seemed unaffected by the war and the society in which they lived.

The day before Tarō left for Kyoto, their grandfather Yasumasa took Jirō with him to visit a fisherman at Misaki Nishihama where they asked for six sea bream for a special farewell dinner that evening. On the way back from Nishihama, Jirō heard from his grandfather that his mother would remarry. Yasumasa spoke of the circumstances that made it necessary for Hisako to remarry. As he listened to his grandfather, Jirō felt some vague anxiety about the future. Apparently Yasumasa had already discussed the matter with Tarō. After they finished dinner that evening, Yasumasa called Hisako and the boys to his room and once again explained to the boys why their mother had to remarry. Their grandmother, Sumie, was also there. Hisako sat with her head bowed.

"Tarō and Jirō, I know this is hard for both of you, but really, there is nothing else I can do." Hisako kept her eyes on the floor as she spoke.

"No one knows whether Kyŏng-hyo Yi is alive or dead. And although the special detectives, who have been searching for some kind of link between the Iwami family and Yi, have backed off now, they are still watching us from a distance. For Hisako to get married would, in a sense, relieve us from that pressure. Hisako will be relieved and you boys' own future will not be so uncertain, so from that standpoint, she just has to get married, don't you agree?" said Yasumasa.

"Please stop crying mother," replied Tarō, "It was just about a year ago that we overheard grandfather urging you to remarry. Both of us are grown up and we understand the suffering you have gone through, mother, during the past year while you were deciding to remarry."

From the way he spoke, this might be taken as a criticism of his mother. Grandma Sumie turned to Tarō and said, "You are too clever for your own good." Jirō could not tell what his brother was thinking or how he felt about this matter, but he realized that they would no longer have their gentle mother with them. Hisako's new home was in Odawara, it was an old family named Shinjō that was in the wholesale fabric business in Nihonbashi just as the Iwami family was.

Again Yasumasa spoke, "The children in the new family are all grown up, and you will be free to go there any time you like to visit your mother."

"We hope our mother will always be beautiful, and will hope to meet her sometimes. Perhaps when I come back from Kyoto for my holidays, I will go for a stroll in Odawara and there on the street I will unexpectedly run into my beautiful mother. Even just the thought of it makes me happy." Tarō spoke so that they could not tell whether he was joking or not.

The next day he left for Kyoto. Hisako and Shizuko saw him off as far as Matsuwa. Jirō accompanied him as far as Ōfuna. It was a rainy day and the coast of the Bōsō Peninsula was shrouded in haze. Tsurugigasaki was awash with waves.

"Jirō, is there anything you believe in?" asked Tarō as they waited on the platform of Ōfuna Station.

"No. I don't believe in anything in particular."

"The only thing I personally can believe in is beauty." Tarō gazed into the distance. From where they were sitting they could see about half the great Ōfuna Kannon statue on the mountain in front of the station. Wild cherry blossoms in the rain gave the slope of the mountain a pale color.

"Tarō, for the past year both of us have been thinking only of one thing—when mother would be leaving. I think this saved us from a terrible shock last night. Thank you."

"What about you? Will you be able to get along by yourself if I am not here?"

"No problem, I'm already a third year student. If possible I would like to finish middle school and go on to the Third Higher School also. I don't know if I will be able to do as well as you have, but I don't intend to complain. You spent your time playing the piano, but for me, well, I joined the *kendō** club. If I ever feel frustrated, I plan to get straightened out by getting myself beaten with a bamboo practice sword."

"Good for you. I will go to Kyoto with an easy mind."

Having seen his brother off, Jirō stopped by his uncle's house in Kamakura, picked up from his aunt a book of Nō chants for his grandfather, and returned to Tsurugi-gasaki. He boarded the bus that went around Takeyama and changed at Misaki. He got off at Matsuwa and looking at the white lighthouse, his eyes filled with tears for the first time. Now, at last, he realized the extent to which he had always relied on his brother. Then it occurred to him, 'I can rely on my brother, but who does my brother rely on?' He realized that ultimately he would have to rely on himself alone.

During the month that remained until Hisako left, Jirō saw as little of his mother as possible. She decided to leave on the first holiday in May. On that day Jirō went to school for *kendō* practice and returned home only after dark. He did not want to be there when his mother left.

Since before the War there had been a shellfish dealer in Misaki who always had stacks of abalone, clams, and turbot piled up in front of his store fresh from the holding tank. Jirō ordered two large abalone and twenty clams and had them put in a plastic bag. It was after four o'clock when he boarded the bus for Zushi which went around Hayama.

No sooner had the bus started than he began to think once more about Tsurugigasaki. His thoughts went back to the time he was fifteen when he was trying to take care of everything for himself.

Tarō sent letters about twice a month from Kyoto. Invariably there was another letter addressed to Shizuko in the same envelope. Jirō learned a lot from his brother in their exchange of letters. The philosophy of life expressed in Tarō's letters was more advanced than one would expect of a seventeen year old. Jirō was inspired to read the letters over and over again. Jirō occasionally thought of the position they had been placed in and wondered if anyone else's situation was so uncertain. He came to understand his brother's feeling when he said the only thing he could believe in was beauty.

Tarō returned to Tsurugigasaki for the summer vacation. Shortly after nine o'clock one morning in the middle of July they received a telegram saying, "Arriving Ōfuna, five o'clock; request bath, food, fish, abalone." As he read this Jirō called to mind his brother's healthy face. Getting money from his grandfather, Jirō went to Misaki to buy abalone.

Jirō had no idea what kind of letters were being exchanged by his brother and Shizuko. His only role was to pass along to Shizuko the additional letter that was always included in the one he received. "If I lose you, I'll die!" There still remained the memory of Shizuko's high, beautiful voice piercing the roar of the wind and the waves. It was beautifully naive, but bordering on insanity.

Jirō did not retain any clear memory of how they spent that summer. He stayed away from Tarō and Shizuko. He remembered spending the greater part of each day gazing at the sea and the sky and studying for his college entrance examinations. He did recall that in the middle of August he spent a week at school at a *kendō* workshop where the fencing master recognized that his skill placed him beyond the first grade.

The Pacific War began on December eighth that year. In the midst of all the excitement caused by the outbreak of the war, Jirō diligently studied for his entrance examinations and practiced *kendō*.

Tarō did not return home during the winter holiday. Early in the new year of 1942, Jirō participated in a *kendō* examination held at the Yokosuka Police Station. By defeating three people of the second grade, he skipped over the first grade and was certified at the second grade.

Tarō did not return home during the spring holidays
either. In April Shizuko returned to Kamakura and her
own school, but in June, shortly after her father, Naoto,
was sent to the front, Shizuko and her mother, Haruko,
again came to Tsurugigasaki. Haruko's reason for the
move was that it would be better to live in the country
where fish and vegetables were plentiful than in the city
where they were scarce. Simply by throwing out a
fishing line a person could catch enough fish so that a
family could live and there were places where one could
gather several kinds of seaweed when the tide was out.
Since Shizuko was attending the Ōtsu Women's School,
it was just as convenient to go from Tsurugigasaki.

Shortly after Haruko and Shizuko came, Shizuko's elder brother, Kenkichi, also came to live with them. He
had failed the Army physical examination, graduated
from a private university in Tokyo, and worked in a
right wing publishing company, but he had quit that job
to become a leader in a branch of the Dawn Society, a
patriotic organization that had been established in Kanagawa Prefecture. He was the only son of Uncle Naoto
and would inevitably inherit the store in Nihonbashi,
but at some point he had gone wrong. Consequently, after Naoto left for the front, Yasumasa would occasionally go to Nihonbashi to keep an eye on things. Since the
head clerk had worked in the store since he was a child,
there was no difficulty about managing the business.

Jirō, living at Tsurugigasaki, did not know very much
about his cousin Kenkichi who was six years his senior.
Kenkichi lived at the Dawn Society headquarters in
Yokohama, coming to Tsurugigasaki only about once

every three days. Soon he was wearing their khaki uniform and black shirts. Jirō never really found out what he was doing. One morning when Kenkichi left the house in his Dawn Society uniform, Yasumasa watched him leave and Jirō heard him mutter, "That idiot!"

Tarō returned home for the summer vacation that year, but after ten days went back to Kyoto. On the day he left, the two brothers took a walk in Odawara. Tarō had suggested the walk. Although he was reluctant to go and visit their mother in her new home, Jirō hoped they might accidentally meet her on the street. He felt that Tarō undoubtedly had the same thought. The brothers spent two hours wandering aimlessly about the streets of the town.

"I don't think she would mind if we went to visit her at the Shinjō house, but —" As he spoke, Jirō looked at the row of houses behind their white earthen walls reflected in the waters of a canal. They had just passed the Shinjō home which had latticed windows in the earthen wall.

"No, let's not. It's silly. It is enough just to know that our mother lives in that house on this street. It would be all right for us, but put yourself in mother's position. We would leave behind some feeling of bitterness if we went to visit. I understand how mother feels. By the way, have you ever felt any resentment for our father who abandoned us? Be honest now."

"I never thought about it."

"You never thought about it? A man who would go off and not leave his wife and children any clue of what happened to him certainly must have a strong will; that's what I think. These days, in fact, I may even have some

25

respect for father for being able to do that."

They walked toward Odawara Station.

"Are you returning to Kyoto early on account of that black shirt?"

"That has something to do with it—I'll tell you a secret. I am going to Korea. I want to find out if our grandmother in Taegu knows anything about what happened to father. Uncle Kyŏng-myŏng said that there was no sense in going, but still—During the holiday I visited Uncle Kyŏng-myŏng in Maizuru. While I was there I heard a number of things. Yasumasa's father, that is our maternal great-grandfather, opened a fabric store in Taegu early in the Meiji* period. He set his daughter up to manage the store after her marriage failed. It turns out that Yasumasa's sister is our father's mother. This woman served as a concubine to some Korean aristocrat at the end of the Yi Dynasty. Uncle Kyŏng-myŏng did not know what kind of transactions took place, but apparently great-grandfather Iwami was a businessman with close political connections. Our Korean grandfather is the one who sent his two boys to the Army and Navy academies. I suspect that father's disappearance will turn out to have been entirely planned by our grandfather. I expect that his idea was to train people who could serve Korea. This is just my theory, but—"

"What did Uncle Kyŏng-myŏng say about all this?"

"The conversation never got that far."

"So how did father and mother meet?"

"During the time father was attending the Army Academy he often came to Kamakura, and I suspect that it must have been at that time that some tender feelings began to develop between them. After all, we have any number of photographs taken in Kamakura while he was attending the Army Academy so the chances are that is what happened. It means he took his cousin for his wife. This may be an odd thing to say, but when I think about Shizuko and me it seems odd that we, too, are cousins. It is like an echo of the relationship between father and mother.

"I want to ask you something. Father has equal parts of Japanese and Korean blood in his veins; do you think that he has the same love for his country that a pure Korean has?"

"I don't know. But somehow I think that he probably could not. We live in a hybrid world, nothing is ever clear cut. The inner movements of a person with mixed blood are like the movement of parallels. If you have two parallel lines, they will never cross no matter how far you extend them. The world is composed of that kind of hybrid, always side by side, but never meeting. What made you suddenly bring up something like that?"

"I was just thinking about the time you said that beauty is the only thing one can believe in."

"Ah. I see. For some people beauty is probably a terrible thing, but for me it is the only thing I can rely on. I detest the Japanese and I detest the Koreans; but I also love the Japanese and I love the Koreans. I have the blood of the oppressor and the blood of the oppressed flowing in me in equal parts, and that conflict will go on forever. It exhausts me and in the end brings nothing but emptiness and despair. I think of having mixed blood as a kind of sin. At times like that, the only thing I can turn to is a painting or a line of poetry. I hit the piano keys. Sound comes out. In a moment the sound is gone. Nevertheless, that sound pierces my being just as though a nail is being driven in. That is the kind of world I can believe in most honestly. I still feel that way, of course and I doubt if I will ever change. How about you?"

"I guess I'm the same as you. But I am different in one respect; if I am sent off to the war, I will go without saying a word. But I plan to go on studying literature and I have a feeling that the time will come when I can love people. I had the feeling recently as I read *Tonio Kröger*. It is a novel depicting the conflict between life and art, but the thing that impressed me most was that Tonio is mixed blooded."

"I have read it, too."

Coming out in front of Odawara Station, the brothers found a restaurant where they went to eat the box lunches they had brought with them.

"You be careful of that black shirt," said Tarō interrupting his lunch.

"I do not think there is much he can do to me."

"It was wrong for someone like that ever to have been born. You can't be too careful with him. It could very well be that there is a strain of insanity in the Iwami family."

"What? Is there any real proof of that?"

"That black shirt is proof enough. He's not normal. Uncle Kyŏng-myŏng told me that there was some insanity a few generations ago, but he did not know any of the details."

Tarō boarded the Kyoto-bound train.

Autumn came and a letter arrived from Tarō. He wrote that he had learned nothing in Korea of their father's whereabouts.

When the new school term began in September, it turned out that Jirō took the same bus to school as Shizuko. Letters did not come from Tarō as regularly as they had before, and when they did come, he asked for money. Jirō did not know what was going on between Tarō and Shizuko, but there was no doubt that Shizuko trusted Tarō. Since Shizuko had been out of school for a year, she repeated her senior year of middle school and in the spring of 1943 entered Tokyo Women's College. At the same time Jirō qualified for the Literature Department of the Third Higher School in Kyoto. Since he took the entrance examination in Tokyo, he did not have a chance to meet his brother, but after the spring holiday they set out together for Kyoto.

Tarō had markedly changed since the previous summer. There was an aura of decadence about him, and the way he looked at things was much more cynical than before. During his stay at Tsurugigasaki he did not exchange a word with his cousin Kenkichi. Jirō did not know what was going on between Tarō and Shizuko apart from the fact that they had gone to Tokyo together one day.

At Kyoto, Jirō went to live at his brother's boarding house. The boarding house was at Shishigatani and Tarō urged him to stay there as the school dormitories were already running short of food. Tarō also advised him, "There is no telling how long you will be able to continue your studies. Any day now the literature students may be sent to Osaka to work in the factories."

Before Jirō had been in school a full month, he was ordered to withdraw. On a day they were having target practice with live ammunition, he shot the officer attached to their school in the left thigh with a bullet from his Model 38 rifle, and it took two weeks for the officer to recover. Even before that Jirō had not gotten along with this officer, a major named Kusuda. According to the family register, Tarō and Jirō were the illegitimate children of Hisako Iwami, and Yi was their acknowledged father. No one knew why Yi did not enter his wife and children on his own family register. After Hisako was married into the Shinjō family, her name was dropped from the register and Tarō became the head of the family. Jirō supposed Major Kusuda had seen the transcript of his family register that he had submitted when he entered school. One day Jirō was called to Major Kusuda. The major looked at him and said, "Well, this is an unusual family background!" He was referring to the fact that they had been mixed blooded for two generations. The names of his acknowledged father's parents were entered on the register. "I have only been at this school since April—what about your older brother who is listed here; where is he?"

"He is a third year student here."

The major stood there for a time looking from the register to Jirō and back again then said, "Koreans are coming up in the world these days; aren't you fortunate you have some Japanese blood in you. Do your best!" Jirō did not understand what the major meant by this, but he detested the man. He had encountered Japanese like this all his life. He was lucky he had not been asked about his father.

One morning about a week later they had target practice with live ammunition. From his middle school days Jirō had always been clumsy with guns. As he lay prone on the rifle range, his gun aimed at the target, the major shouted, "What kind of position is that?" Jirō knew from experience there was going to be trouble. During his middle school years he had often been scolded by his military instructor for his poor positioning. He tried to correct himself.

"Where do you think you're pointing that gun?" screamed the officer. As he moved to correct his posture, Jirō had inadvertently pointed the gun at the major.

"Look out! You idiot! You Korean! Point that thing over here. Point it this way." With long strides the major went to the target and rapped it with his sword.

Some of his classmates were waiting for the order to take their positions and some were in the same posture as Jirō and he could feel that all of them who were lined up to the left of him were watching. It may have been natural at this point for his thoughts to flash back to his childhood when the fishermen's children had picked quarrels with him at Tsurugigasaki Elementary School. There was no time to think. It only took a moment to squeeze the trigger. The major toppled over with a strange cry. Feeling vicious, Jirō picked up his rifle and walked to where the major lay. Opening the breech of the gun, he ejected the spent cartridge, closed it, and pointed the muzzle at the major's chest.

"I'm going to kill you! I have four shots left."

With a surge of rage he pulled back the hammer. He felt a curious sense of sadness as he realized how easy it would be to pull the trigger again and a bullet would surely pierce this man's heart. The major clutched his left leg and tried to speak. Jirō stood over the major who lay there looking up with eyes like a dog's, trying to say something. Jirō felt emptiness, despair, and a strange sense of impatience. Images formed in his mind—his brother's face, the wall around the house of the Shinjō family in Odawara, the latticed windows reflected in the canal. Throwing down his rifle, he turned his back on the rifle range and walked toward the school. His breast gradually began to fill with remorse as he walked. Although he personally had always been aware of his own heritage, he had never since middle school been reminded of it point blank by the people around him, and yet from time to time he did encounter the gaze of a person who seemed to see him as an alien. He had always managed to keep himself under control before, why had this happened now? He was definitely sorry.

The only thing that kept the matter from becoming a criminal case were the measures taken by a number of his teachers. Also in his favor was the fact that a majority of his classmates testified that the major was at fault. The major's opinion was that since the matter was taken care of on campus, the assailant must be expelled. On the day Jirō was advised to withdraw from school, his professor asked if he would be willing to pay a visit to the major who was recuperating at home. Jirō refused. His hatred for the major had been dispelled, but he still felt the man was disgusting.

"A friend of mine holds a professorship in Western history at Waseda University," said his professor. "If you want, you can try to get into some other school next year, but for the time being, you should go to Waseda. I'll write to my friend and see if we can simply have you transfer to Waseda."

Jirō took the letter, thanked his teacher, and returned to the boarding house in Shishigatani where he found his brother stretched out on the floor reading a book.

"You seem to have a more violent temper than I supposed. You have never done anything like this before; I was quite surprised," said Tarō with a sarcastic smile.

"I have a feeling that something like this is going to happen again in the future, only next time we won't be so lucky."

"Are you sorry for what you did? A person who cannot compromise has no choice, does he? You will have plenty of time to think about it while fishing at Tsurugigasaki. Actually, it will be better for you to go to Waseda since you are going to study literature."

Jirō left Kyoto with bitter memories. He was able to transfer to the Second Higher School at Waseda University, but that year was a gloomy one. Early in December they began sending students to the front, and at the end of the month they lowered by one year the age of people subject to the draft.

In February of the following year, 1944, the draft law was enforced in Korea and Uncle Kyŏng-myŏng in Maizuru was reassigned to instruct the Koreans who were at the Naval Academy in Yokosuka. When he came to Tsurugigasaki to say hello, he had been promoted to lieutenant commander. Kyŏng-myŏng was not married and moved about from navy base to navy base; Jirō felt he could not understand his Uncle's way of life. Tarō entered the Science Department at Kyoto University and returned home at the end of March, but after a few days he abruptly left again for Kyoto. He did not come home during the summer holiday. At the end of August there were orders for student civilian labor and when the new term began in the autumn, Jirō was sent to a factory in Kawasaki. In November the B-29's began bombing Tokyo. It was even gloomier than the year before. There was a battery of anti-aircraft guns on the edge of the Miura Peninsula which had become a fortified area. Even Tsurugigasaki had acquired anti-aircraft and heavy artillery batteries since the previous summer. The lighthouse no longer lit up the sea at night. Shizuko was assigned to work at Kawasaki in the same factory as Jirō, but she came down with another attack of pleurisy and spent her time at home as an invalid in Tsurugigasaki.

"There haven't been any letters from Kyoto recently, have there?" said Shizuko one day toward the end of the year. She was gaunt and only her eyes were large. Tarō, however, did not return home during the winter holiday either and finally 1945 came around.

With the arrival of March there was also a notice that his uncle, Naoto, had died in battle. Early in April, Yasumasa, Sumie, and Haruko went to Yokohama to receive his remains and they had a memorial service performed. Naoto had gone to the front as a private first class and he returned as a dead corporal. Tarō returned home on the day of the memorial service. He stayed briefly at Tsurugigasaki, and then left again for Kyoto. During this time Jirō was going back and forth to work in the factory and did not know if anything had happened between Tarō and Shizuko.

After that, Kenkichi, the black shirt, formed the National Loyal Defense League and went around the Miura Peninsula teaching people how to use bamboo spears. If the American army invaded, he expected to turn the tide of the war with bamboo spears. Small American aircraft from Iwo Jima carried out raids, and although the batteries on the Miura Peninsula continued to fire at them, the American planes rarely went down.

The store in Nihonbashi had nothing left to sell, so Yasumasa closed it and spent all his time at Tsurugigasaki reading old Nō texts. After Naoto's death the family did not talk much, and each day continued as gloomy as the next. The newspapers had captions saying that wild grasses could be eaten and people were exhorted to serve such things as nettles and spiderwort. Seeing this in the paper, Yasumasa was heard to mutter, 'It won't be long now.'

Shizuko was clearly concerned about Tarō's safety, but on August seventh he returned home.

3

In September the house and surrounding area were alive with the incessant cries of cicadas, but it was cool there both in the morning and in the evening when a fresh breeze blew through it.

Having gone back to visit Tsurugigasaki, Jirō spent each day immersed in thoughts of the past. The gloomy part, buried in the crevasses of his mind, did not diminish. Even now, seventeen years later, it was still painful. How often in the past he had wanted to escape that gloom, and eventually there came a time when he felt nothing at all. His grandfather, Yasumasa, had never once suggested that they visit the graves at Tsurugigasaki. Indeed, Yasumasa had immediately agreed to sell the place when he was approached in the spring of 1946 by someone from nearby Uraga who had a steel mill and who had made a lot of money during the War.

Jirō tried to think that this meeting with his father would be an opportunity to rid himself of these gloomy memories, but all he could remember of his father was the man as he had looked when Jirō was eleven years old. Even when he tried thinking back over the intervening twenty-five years, it did not seem likely that there would be any adequate resolution. There was no course open to him but to understand realistically the great changes that had beset the Iwami family just as the war ended. He thought back over the months and years he had spent at Tsurugigasaki. He also tried to imagine how his father and mother had met. His father and mother were cousins, just as Tarō and Shizuko were cousins. It may be a trivial matter to think about, but he recalled how Tarō, walking down the streets of Odawara had said, "I wonder if it is just a coincidence that we, too, are cousins?" Jirō felt a mysterious fate was directing their lives. This feeling had been especially strong in the past six years since he had been lecturing on medieval Japanese literature at a private university.

Jirō read an article in the newspaper that said an important Korean official would stop in Japan for two days on his way to the United States. The article mentioned Yi's name and, as Jirō had imagined, he was a military official. It turned out that the group would arrive at the airport on the afternoon of the thirteenth.

Jirō took the newspaper to his grandfather's room.

"Should we meet him at the airport?" asked Yasumasa glancing over the article and taking off his glasses.

"I think it would be just as well not to meet him at the airport—"

"Why is that?"

"I don't know, but somehow that's the way I feel. I guess I am anxious after all these years. Don't you think it would be just as well to wait for father to come here? That's what I was thinking."

Yasumasa thought for a moment and said, "All right. Let's do that, then."

At ten o'clock on the morning of the fourteenth, Yi visited the Iwami family. The previous evening a woman had telephoned to say that he would arrive at ten o'clock the following morning. It was Friday and Jirō had a lecture to give, but he stayed home from school and waited for his father to come.

Shortly after ten o'clock he heard the sound of a car pulling up in front of the house. Hearing the car stop, Jirō went out and walked slowly toward the front gate.

A large, black car was parked at the foot of the stone

steps and two men wearing suits were climbing the stairs. The man in the lead was an imposing figure with a sunburned face and a white forehead. Jirō realized at a glance that this resulted from wearing an army hat. Despite a separation of twenty-five years, this instant of realization was perhaps due to the special relationship between father and son. Jirō felt all these things as he watched the men climb the steps.

When he reached the gate, Yi looked at Jirō and said, "Jirō?"

"Yes."

Jirō lowered his gaze, and silently inviting his father in through the gate, led the way to the house. Yasumasa and Michiko met them at the door. Both groups bowed silently. When the young man accompanying Yi had deposited his package in the entry hall, he said something to Yi in Korean, saluted, turned on his heel, and went out. Although Jirō had understood Korean when he was a child in Taegu, he could not now understand what they had said.

Yasumasa silently led the way along the corridor followed by Yi and Jirō.

Meeting like this after twenty-five years, it was very quiet as everyone was absorbed in his own thoughts. This was the first time Yasumasa had seen Yi in thirty years.

After they had all been seated, Yi's first words were, "It's been a long time. The house has gotten older, but otherwise it has not changed a bit since the twenties."

"How old are you now?" asked Yasumasa.

"Fifty-eight."

"You're still young, then. I'm already seventy-nine."

"Are you? You certainly don't look it."

"Many things have happened — I never thought we would ever meet again like this."

"Thank you for all you have done."

"I feel as though I have watched the passing of history with my own eyes. Jirō and I are the only ones left now."

"I expect there are many things you would like to say."

For a while they sat in silence, then Yasumasa said, "I haven't once blamed you for the things that have happened. Even if I find out what kind of life you have led, it won't change the past. You were my nephew before you became my son-in-law. This close blood relationship may have made me generous. As things turned out, you have followed the way that was right for you. But your position is different now and we cannot have the old, easy intimacy any longer. That is history as far as I am concerned. I think I have come to terms with history."

"That's generous of you."

As Jirō listened to the conversation between his father and grandfather, he wondered what kind of history would include two generations of mixed blood. He wondered if the day would ever come when the fact of being of mixed blood would be understood in Japan. As he sat there before this man who was important in his own country, who concealed iron in his soul, but whom Jirō could no longer call father, he thought back and remembered the expression on his brother's face on the street in Odawara when Tarō had said, "Being of mixed blood is a kind of sin."

Yi said that both of his parents who had been living in Taegu had died during the Korean War. Tarō's death was also brought up, but Hisako was never mentioned. Yi would depart the next morning for America, but he would be returning to Korea in December and, if possible, would like to stop again in Japan at that time. He was taking back to Korea a group of young officers who had been training in the United States. Bringing out the package left by his young companion, he said, "Here's a present." It was *ginseng*.

He called to the young man who was waiting in the car, and after they had eaten lunch, Jirō took his father to Tsurugigasaki to show him around. The young man drove and Jirō sat in the back seat with his father.

"How long will it take to get there?" asked Yi.

"I expect it will be less than an hour by car. I have not gone back there since we left Tsurugigasaki. I have only gloomy memories of the place. When I received your letter in August, I went to visit the graves there for the first time."

"Please tell me what happened. After all, there is nothing I can say about the matter since I shirked my duty as a father."

"Neither Tarō nor I ever held a grudge against you, father. In the summer of 1942, Tarō went over to Taegu to see if he could find out anything about you."

"I heard that he had been there when I returned to Taegu after the war."

"Mother remarried the year before that."

"I heard about that too. I am sorry it had to be that way. Tell me about Tarō."

Yi closed his eyes and waited for Jirō to speak. Inside
the car it was cool with air conditioning, and the sound
of the motor could not be heard. Jirō took them on the
road that led around Hayama.

At ten o'clock on the morning of August seventh, 1945,
the tide was out and Jirō was at the edge of the beach
fishing. After the factory in Kawasaki had been burned
in an air raid, he had been sent to work in a factory in
Yokohama, but it, too, was completely destroyed in the
massive B-29 raid of May twenty-ninth, and he ended up
attending school again until they could find another
place for him to work. But the American planes came
every day from Iwo Jima in uninterrupted waves and
since the trip from Tsurugigasaki to Waseda and back
took a full day, he gave up school. Like most of his
classmates, he was a student in name only and ignored
his studies; the government could do nothing but urge
the people to eat weeds and go to war. Even the factories
to which others were assigned no longer had any work
to do. There were no raw materials for manufacturing
products. His friends who were assigned to work in the
Yokosuka Navy Yards said they had no work to do and
spent each day digging air raid shelters.

Even though there were fields of vegetables at Tsurugigasaki, there was no longer much to harvest in them.
In Jirō's family they had to serve wild grasses about once
every three days. These were not the succulent wild
grasses of early spring, however, but rather the tough,
woody stalks of mid-summer. Instead of onions they had

wild leeks that had gone to seed. Still, they were more fortunate than those living in Tokyo because at least they had wild grasses to eat. The only thing that was plentiful was fish. There was one point on the beach where the shore dropped off abruptly and the current swirled swiftly. There, depending on the season, one could catch black bream, ishimochi, mackerel, greenling, mullet, and mebaru. Haruko, whose husband had been killed, would look at the calendar and, on days when there was a Buddhist prohibition, tell Jirō he was not to catch fish, but Yasumasa said that necessity knows no laws and told him to go ahead and fish.

Every day Jirō put out his line, gazed at Bōsō and wondered what his brother was doing.

As always his cousin Kenkichi went around in his Dawn Society uniform and carried a bamboo spear. He was a gaunt, energetic figure. From somewhere he had acquired a supply of sake and spent his time drinking with his friends. On the breast of his khaki uniform he had sewn in red thread the emblem of the Dawn Society on the right and the Japanese flag on the left. He practiced with his spear until it was well worn and sweat-stained. As the war situation became graver for Japan, Kenkichi began acting very strangely and rarely spoke to the family. To Jirō who had become as negligent about things as any other student, his cousin's words and actions were more than odd, they were grotesque. Whenever Yasumasa saw Kenkichi, he would look pained and say, "That fool!"

On the morning of August seventh, Jirō was fishing at the edge of the beach. He had caught two beautiful red scorpionfish. Although they were a kind of mebaru, the local fishermen called the red ones scorpionfish and the blackish-brown ones mebaru. It was unusual to catch red ones. Jirō wondered if this meant his brother was coming home. On several occasions in the past he had caught red fish on the day his brother returned home; Jirō took this as a good omen. The fish he had caught were about twenty centimeters long, but he still had to catch about three more fish the same size. Since staple foods could no longer be bought, fish was their main source of nourishment.

With the thought, 'Tarō may be returning home today,' he also became concerned about Shizuko. Since early in July she had stopped eating, saying food made her nauseous. One evening Jirō caught a glimpse of Haruko questioning Shizuko. Shizuko had refused to answer and looked away. A few days later Haruko asked Jirō about the relationship between Tarō and Shizuko. He could only answer that he knew nothing about it. A few days later when he went to a nearby farmhouse to get some vegetables, the farm woman asked if it was true that the young lady in his family was pregnant. Jirō thought to himself, 'So that's it.'

Fishing boats dotted the Uraga channel and Sagami Bay. They had been instructed not to go too far from shore. Previously there had been a constant churning of battleships, cruisers, and destroyers in and out of Yokosuka, but recently that had suddenly stopped and only once in a while would he see a seriously damaged ship being towed into the harbor by a small boat. In April, Tarō had told him the war was nearly over, and as

he looked out at the ocean, he decided that it was probably true.

"Oi, Jirō!" Turning in response to this shout, he saw his
brother standing at the top of the cliff, waving.

"Yo, Tarō! I caught two red scorpionfish."

"I'll come right down." Tarō disappeared and presently
came out of the ravine onto the beach.

"How long will you be home this time?" asked Jirō as
his brother approached.

"I will be here for a while – Jirō, the war will soon be
over. Perhaps it will be over within a couple of days."

"Are you sure?"

"You probably haven't heard about it yet, but yesterday morning at about eight o'clock a terrible thing happened. They dropped a bomb on Hiroshima – it's called
an atomic bomb and it works by smashing atoms. It has
so much power that the entire city was destroyed by one
bomb. I heard about it yesterday morning at ten o'clock
when I was in the theoretical physics lab, and I came
home right away. I had good train connections and got
here fast, but the point is that the war is definitely going
to be over now."

"Is it?" It suddenly occurred to Jirō that he might have
a chance to see his father again once the war was over.
Somehow it did not really feel like the war was going to
be over. "Have you seen Shizuko yet?"

"Yes."

"Did you talk to her?"

"Yes, I did – When the war is over I plan to take Shizuko back to Kyoto with me."

"Didn't Aunt Haruko have anything to say about that?"

"I haven't seen her yet. Apparently she has gone to Nishiyato to buy rice. Anyway, I'll talk to her tonight or tomorrow."

"She just bought rice yesterday."

"It doesn't really matter. What I want to know is whether or not Black Shirt has changed."

"He's even crazier than before."

"What does that bastard do? Where does he go every day?"

"In June the government passed the National Voluntary Military Service Law. Every day he goes to elementary and middle school playgrounds where he rounds up the men and has them practice jabbing straw dummies with their bamboo spears. He goes around teaching that. I saw him one time teaching them at Shimoura Elementary School."

"He's some kind of warped genius."

"Why do you say that?"

"I admire his pointless howl. He is just the right sort of person to inspire patriotism when the country shows signs of going into its death throes."

"It's a kind of insanity."

"We have been bystanders in this war because we are not pure Japanese. In that respect I am thankful for my blood."

"I am not able to be a bystander in the way you are. The fact is that one of our uncles died in the war and another is in the Navy. Besides, if it had not been for the war, our father might not have disappeared. Recently Uncle Kyŏng-myŏng came to visit by car and brought a load of meat from the Navy Yards, but what will happen when the war ends?"

"Who did you hope would win the war?"

"I never considered that, but I never thought I wouldn't mind if Japan were defeated."

"I have been thinking all along that whether Japan wins or loses has nothing to do with me. For a person who is caught in the middle, this is the only way to think."

"What about our father and Uncle Kyŏng-myŏng?"

"It's worse for them than it is for us. They will always be half one thing and half the other. The right hand will hate the left hand and the left hand will hate the right. This conflict will continue. Both sides needed support so one went over to the enemy and the other stayed with the Japanese. That's all there is to it. It will make us feel better if we think of mixed bloods as a special new race.

On the seashore behind them the midday sun was reflected on the water and they were engulfed in suffocating heat.

In the morning newspapers on August eighth was an article on the new kind of bomb that had been dropped on Hiroshima. The article said that damage in the city appeared severe, and that from now on people should pay attention to air raids consisting of a small squadron of planes and that if one of the new kind of bombs was dropped, injury could be avoided simply by wearing white overalls and if one were in an air raid shelter, one would be all right.

"Incredible. What kind of idiots are they?" laughed Tarō loudly as he looked at the morning paper while eating breakfast.

"Who do you think you're calling an idiot?" demanded Kenkichi.

"The government leaders and the people at the Imperial Headquarters."

"Why?"

"It says here that you can avoid injury simply by wearing white overalls. The bomb they dropped on Hiroshima two days ago was just not that simple. One bomb completely destroyed the whole city. The way things are now, it would only take three or four of these bombs to destroy Tokyo completely."

"Are you saying you hope that's what happens?"

"Listen Kenkichi, don't put words in my mouth."

"After breakfast I have something to say to you and Jirō. When you are done eating, go down to the beach and wait for me."

"If you have something to say, say it here, now!" demanded Yasumasa.

"I can't. It has to do with these two brothers. It's just between the three of us."

"You watch your language. I don't know what you have to say to Tarō and Jirō, but you can say it here. I won't allow just the three of you to talk together!" Yasumasa was clearly angry.

"It will be all right, grandfather. No doubt he wants to reveal to us his secret strategy for winning the war by jabbing one another with bamboo spears," Tarō spoke this way to relieve the tension that had come over them, but Jirō could not tell if he was being sarcastic or joking. For some reason, his grandmother, aunt, and Shizuko sat silently looking at their laps.

After they had finished eating, the brothers went down the slope of Tsurugigasaki to the beach. Tarō was whistling.

"Did you talk to grandfather and Aunt Haruko about Shizuko?" asked Jirō.

"I talked to them last night. They are resigned to the fact that they have no choice but to do it my way. Apparently Black Shirt is the only one who opposes it."

"If that's what he wants to talk about, why would he have called me down here, too?"

"There must be something else on his mind; he went on ahead and is waiting for us."

"I certainly doubt if he would try to stab us with his bamboo spear, but wouldn't it be better for all of us if you didn't always go around skewering people with your tongue? I remember what you said some time ago, that several generations back there was a streak of insanity in the Iwami family."

"I'm not worried. You ought to think about what happened to you in Kyoto. Don't start anything, no matter what that bastard says. After all, if there is a streak of insanity in the Iwami family, you and I have that blood flowing in us too."

When the brothers reached the bottom of the ravine and came out onto the sun-drenched beach, there stood Kenkichi in his black-shirted uniform.

"I have something important to say," said Kenkichi looking at the brothers.

Jirō felt he could see a strange glint in Kenkichi's eyes, but perhaps it was only his imagination.

"The money you two brought with you from Korea

was used up long ago. My father died in the war, we no longer have any business left, and the family is without money. You two are both grown up now, so I want you to leave. Now that my father is gone, I am the head of this household and as head of the family I cannot go on supporting you two forever."

"Listen, in the summer of '42, I got a substantial amount of money from my grandmother in Korea," replied Tarō. "I left it in the care of Yasumasa. We may be a burden to you in other ways, but we are no trouble financially."

"This is the first I have heard about that, but even so, I want to know when you are going to leave. After all, there is no reason for you to be living with us just because you have money."

"I understand. We will leave very soon. Is that all you have to say?"

"There's one more thing. I will not allow you and Shizuko to be together."

"Oh? And why not?"

"You are cousins. Your father and mother were cousins also. I can't allow it on grounds of heredity."

"I understand your concern, but it's already too late."

"I will make Shizuko have an abortion."

"What if she insists on having the baby?"

"I won't allow it."

"And your only reason for that is because we are cousins? Kenkichi, you will never be able to break up the relationship between Shizuko and me."

"Let me say this very clearly. I will not give my sister to a Korean. You have some Japanese blood in you, but I won't give my sisten to anyone who has the slightest trace of non-Japanese blood. Look at the trouble it causes; my aunt and great aunt have had plenty. I'm talking about your mother who married a Korean and about your grandmother. We must get rid of these bad elements right now!"

"Bad elements? Of course. Listen Kenkichi, you can't keep Shizuko and me apart."

"You cannot be together."

"I tell you, you cannot keep Shizuko and me apart."

"If you really mean that, then I have an idea."

"What kind of idea would you have? You can't keep the two of us apart. We will be leaving here soon. We are grateful to you, but I will take Shizuko when I go."

"I absolutely forbid it! It will cause nothing but disaster for you two to be together. If you two are together, it can only end badly. You mark my words."

"Speak more clearly. It may be disastrous, there may be a bad ending in store, but you, Kenkichi, cannot keep Shizuko and me apart."

"If you try to take Shizuko away, I'll kill you!"

"Go ahead. I'll die anyway, someday. If I lose my life on account of the woman I love, that will be fine with me. I assure you, cousin, there will be no separation between Shizuko and myself."

"Your father was a traitor who deserted the Japanese Army and went over to the enemy. That alone was harmful to Japan; I can never forgive that. I think we have done a lot for you, just by raising the children of a traitor like that. Now, on top of that, you plan to smear the Iwami family with shame; do you think I will let you do that? When you fled here, my late father went to a lot of trouble on your behalf. Have you ever considered that? I said that I will kill you if you take Shizuko with you. I mean it. I will give you ten days. During that time I want you to get your things together and get out!"

When Kenkichi had finished speaking, he left. Jirō watched his uniformed cousin's back as he retreated; he felt a strange bloodthirstiness. Kenkichi's eyes as he talked had definitely not been normal. Jirō realized that he had encountered eyes like that several times in the past, but he could not recall where. When at last the khaki-uniformed figure turned right and disappeared, the feeling that passed through Jirō was that as a person of mixed blood it was his fate to be rejected.

"I didn't expect to be branded and stigmatized by my own relatives. He's a stupid fool," said Tarō sitting down on a stone.

"What do you plan to do?" Jirō sat down next to Tarō and gazed out at the sea. The Bōsō shore opposite was shrouded in mist and in front of them the white-capped waves were smashing themselves to pieces.

"These next few days will be the final crisis of the war. Until then I will just fish. Once the war is over, I will take Shizuko and go to Kyoto. You can stay with us in Kyoto until the autumn school term begins."

"That bastard said he will kill you. I don't think he was kidding."

"You're probably right. But he couldn't kill anyone. Besides, all he can kill is a person; he can't kill the feeling I have within me."

"Tarō — What are you saying?"

"You're worried. We should have enough money left to last us until we are finished with school. Once the war is over, there may be a revaluation of the currency, but we shouldn't have to worry. Go on now, bring the fishing poles. We'll catch some fish for lunch. I want to catch some perch, so bring plenty of fishing line. I'll dig the bait."

Although he still felt some misgivings, Jirō was relieved that his brother had retained his normal thoughts and actions. In order to catch sea perch, they had to drop their hooks to the very bottom of the ocean. When they did this, they often snagged their hooks on the seaweed and fouled their lines. Jirō was relieved that his brother was calm enough to point out that they would need plenty of fishing line.

Just as he was turning into the ravine, he was stopped by Tarō's call, "If anyone at the house asks you what happened, be sure and say it was nothing. We don't want to upset the women. Even if he is a fool, he is still a member of their family."

"I wonder if grandfather would agree with that?"

"It doesn't matter how he feels about it. Don't forget to bring the cigarettes."

As he went under the shadow of the rocks, Jirō recalled the day his mother had decided to remarry, when his grandmother Sumie had looked at Tarō and said, "You are too smart for your own good." Behind this sarcastic gaze, he had sympathy for other people, but this was something no one but his immediate family realized. As he came up from the beach, Jirō saw, on the slope above, Shizuko wearing a straw hat and carrying the fishing poles. She was going down to the beach.

"What's Tarō doing?" she asked in her high, beautiful voice.

"He's down below."

Presently Shizuko came down the slope to where Jirō waited. "What did Kenkichi say to you?"

"Nothing much," Jirō turned and walked back down with her.

"Even if he is my own brother, I think his behavior this morning was inexcusable."

Jirō did not reply.

Tarō was looking out at the sea. Jirō paused a moment looking down at his brother and felt that he was seeing the real Tarō. Behind his sarcastic gaze was sympathy for other people and behind that was this posture. Such was Jirō's feeling.

"Tarō!" called Shizuko, "Grandfather wants to talk to you."

"What about?" asked Tarō turning to face them.

"I don't know. What did my brother say to you?"

"He told us about his plan for fighting the Americans when they invade."

With that Shizuko was silent and walked slowly to where Tarō was standing. They sat down together on the rocks.

"Grandfather said he has something important to tell you. Jirō and I will do the fishing; you go on and hear what he has to say," said Shizuko in a low voice.

Both of them were gazing at the same spot on the ocean. It reminded Jirō of the March day four years earlier just before Tarō left for Kyoto to go to school when they had been sitting exactly like this. He retained in his mind the sound of Shizuko's voice saying, "If I lose you, I will die!" It was a sharp woman's voice that pierced the noise of the wind and the waves. On that occasion they had been sitting just like this.

"You say it's something important? Well, I guess I had better go and see." Tarō got up and walked slowly to the top of the rocks.

"Tarō!" cried Shizuko. As he turned, there was a look of approval in his eyes. Then he turned and walked slowly into the ravine.

"A few days ago I heard something from my brother," said Shizuko a few moments later.

"I'll dig some bait," said Jirō leaving Shizuko's side. He began flipping over small stones looking for bait. He was thinking, 'The whole family has heard about this from Black Shirt several days ago.' Yasumasa's attitude at breakfast confirmed this. No doubt Yasumasa had restrained Kenkichi.

"Why don't you brothers ever complain about things?" Shizuko mused, but Jirō kept silent and continued looking for bait.

"I remember when we were children. Back in the days when your father attended the Army Academy. Tarō was five and you were three. I was four. Tarō was born in Kamakura while your father was at the Academy. Shortly after that he went to Korea where you were born. I learned all this from grandmother. She said that in 1929 your father brought the whole family back to Kamakura. Then, a year later, you went to Korea to stay. It was all very bewildering, and at the time it seemed you were constantly moving about. In my childish heart I felt sad at being separated from you."

"Why are you remembering all those things from the past?" asked Jirō without pausing in his search for bait.

"I don't know. You brothers have had too much sadness in your lives."

"I don't remember much about Kamakura when I was a child; the only thing I remember is that we often went to see the trains."

"Yes, we always went together to the outer gate of the Engakuji Temple to watch the trains go by. All four of us would go. I can't imagine why Kenkichi alone has changed so much."

"It's the times. It won't do any good to complain about it. Neither my brother nor I take these things very seriously. You shouldn't worry about them either, Shizuko."

Presently, Jirō finished preparing their fishing lines and put them out.

Some distance from the shore an aged fisherman was sculling past in his boat. The boat came from Misaki and was heading toward Minami Shimoura. It was a tranquil moment which belied the fact that a war was going on. As he looked up at the empty sky and gazed out at the blue sea, Jirō felt within himself the sadness of summer. There had been moments like this in the past. It was the year his brother had gone to Kyoto and shortly afterwards his mother had gone to Odawara. There were the days he had walked down the road between Matsuwa and Tsurugigasaki, through fields with the heat waves shimmering, when the sadness of spring had pierced his very being. He had no reason to hate Kenkichi. They should be grateful to the Iwami family despite that fact that their father had left a large sum of money with their mother and despite the fact that Tarō received money from his grandmother in Korea. He realized that he had grown very fond of the sea here. He would remember these years and months since they had come to Tsurugigasaki as a period when his brother had looked at things sarcastically, and when he himself had constantly held in check the violence he felt; both of them had been thinking only of triumphing over themselves.

There were nights when he had felt that there was no way to escape and when he had to wonder what kind of violence he would encounter the next day.

Shizuko was looking at the Bōsō Peninsula. Her hair was pushed up under her straw hat, but a few strands were falling down. These stray hairs were being teased by the sea breeze.

"Tarō said he was going to take you back to Kyoto with him."

"What will you do, Jirō?"

"I expect I will find a lodging house in Tokyo."

"I expect grandfather will have something to say about this. How can a person drive away his own blood relatives?"

"Tarō said the war will be over in the next few days. If that happens, other choices will open up."

An air raid siren sounded in the direction of Matsuwa and moments later carrier based planes were in the sky. Nearby anti-aircraft batteries opened fire and it appeared that there was also firing from the Bōsō Peninsula opposite, but no planes fell. All they could hear was the sound of the anti-aircraft shells exploding. Puffs of smoke floated high in the air.

The following day, the ninth of August, they heard on an evening radio report that the new kind of bomb had been dropped on Nagasaki and that the Soviet Union had entered the war. "I was right, the war is over," Tarō murmured to Jirō. When he asked what grandfather had said to him, Tarō laughed and replied, "He told me we won't have to leave here, but I didn't say anything."

It was another five days until the broadcast on the fifteenth announced the end of the war. During this time Tarō and Jirō spent their time fishing. On the twelfth they caught a lot of fish. In the pantry they had two bucketsful of horse mackeral they had caught. It is a rare thing to have such a good day when the tides are just right and the fish are in near the shore.

During this period Jirō noticed that several times Tarō and Shizuko would disappear in the woods behind the house. As Jirō put out his fishing line and gazed at Bōsō, his thoughts went back to Shizuko who had blurted, "If I lose you, I'll die!" He imagined the two of them in the depths of the forest, lonesomely, desperately, losing themselves in each others arms with the sunlight speckling color over them; all he could feel was sadness. After the tenth of August, one could feel that there was a premonition of destruction about them. Jirō wondered if Tarō had given up the idea of taking Shizuko with him because Kenkichi was becoming more wildly fanatical every day. Jirō tried to believe that this was so. Even if Tarō went ahead to Kyoto and Shizuko followed later, Kenkichi would certainly track them down. There was

an incident in Zushi where a man had been killed by
several members of the Dawn Society for advocating op-
position to the war. This happened on the eleventh and
when he heard about it, Jirō remembered the murderous
intent in Kenkichi's eyes when he had threatened to kill
Tarō. Jirō had not understood at the time, but those eyes
expressed an intensity of cruelty and despair he had
never encountered before. Jirō prayed that his brother
would avoid trouble.

4

"So this is Tsurugigasaki," said Yi. He got out of the car
and looked across the valley at the white lighthouse on
the other side.

In autumn, the year the war ended, they had once
again lit the lighthouse whose beacon could be seen
eighteen miles away. Now the lighthouse sparkled in the
late summer sunlight. A large, gray ship was cruising on
Sagami Bay.

"The setting is picturesque, but it is somehow
desolate."

"Yes. During the war it was even more desolate than
this."

Father and son went together to visit the graves.

The area around the graves was even more overgrown
with asters than when Jirō had been there in August.
Under the bright sun, the flowers were blooming in a

bright profusion of white, pink, red, and scarlet.

"The one on the right is Tarō, Shizuko is in the middle, and Uncle Kyŏng-myŏng is on the left. When I think back on it, those days seem like a nightmare."

They walked over the asters and stood in front of the graves.

"Tarō, father has come to pay you a visit." The words came easily and naturally to his lips. Both closed their eyes and clasped their hands in prayer. Then they sat down in front of the graves.

"During the evening of the fourteenth while Tarō and I were talking, we decided to go and visit mother since we would not be coming back here once we left for Kyoto. We decided that I, too, would go to Kyoto and stay for a while at Tarō's lodging house, and then go back to Tokyo or somewhere. On the morning of the fourteenth we had heard definitely that the war was over. We decided that we would both go to Odawara the following afternoon. That day we got up early and went down to the ocean to fish. They say a lot of impatient people like fishing, but it was while fishing during this period that I learned patience. We left Tsurugigasaki at about ten o'clock and got on the train at Kurihama, but Tarō did not seem too happy. About the time the train reached Kamakura, he said, 'Oh, hell! We can't do this,' and got off. I was bewildered by that and got off with him. It was just before noon and the city was silent in anticipation of the Emperor's broadcast. We walked slowly down the main street toward the Hachiman Shrine. We had just come in front of the Kamakura Bookstore when it happened; 'Do you really want to see her?' asked Tarō. Since we had discussed the matter the night before, I replied, 'I'll do whatever you say.' We went into the bookstore and spent some time leafing through books at random, and a short time later went back out. 'Let's go home and pack our things,' said Tarō. We had not yet made a definite decision on when to leave for Kyoto; the problem was how to get railway passes. In those days it was rather difficult for civilians to get railway passes. Tarō suggested we try calling Uncle Kyŏng-myŏng; so we took the train to Yokosuka and called him at the Navy Yards. He told us to wait at the station and a short time later arrived by car. He got three passes on the express train for us. They were for the overnight express on the sixteenth. 'I probably won't be able to leave the Navy Yards,' he said. 'So you two take care of yourselves.' With those words he returned to the base and we went back to Tsurugigasaki."

"Was that the day Tarō was killed?"

"No—It happened the following afternoon. On the sixteenth."

Sitting there surrounded by asters, Jirō heard the sound of waves. Sagami Bay was bathed in September sunlight. He watched the white surf breaking on the sword point of Tsurugigasaki.

"I feel I know how he saw things and what he was thinking at the time. There was a question of whether the end of the war would be good for our future or whether it would mean an even greater burden of uncertainty. There was a general feeling of liberation once the fighting stopped, but it was not something he and I shared. The Korean people rejoiced at the liberation of

Korea, but even that had nothing to do with us. Every day we lived at Tsurugigasaki we had the feeling of having to keep ourselves under control. Tarō was brighter than most people, and he saw the hollowness of everything. In his mind he was constantly brooding about his heritage. As we got off the bus at Matsuwa he told me that even the end of the war had not changed our situation. Since there was no gasoline left, it was one of those busses that ran on charcoal or firewood.

The only thing we thought about as we walked toward Tsurugigasaki was the best way to tell grandfather that we were leaving for Kyoto. The only ones who accepted us as ordinary people were grandfather and Shizuko. Neither Uncle Naoto nor Aunt Haruko nor our grandmother was very fond of us. That was especially true after mother left. People would have considered us social outcasts even if we only had one percent foreign blood in our veins. They were especially hard on Koreans. We seemed to be under a curse quite unrelated to moral considerations. Apart from the main problem of having mixed blood, the fact that we were economically independent was one of the reasons we didn't fit in on either side. We could not blend in with the Japanese nor could we blend in with the Koreans; we had to go on living day after day caught in the middle. In the spring of 1941, Tarō told me that beauty was the only thing he could believe in; that was just before he left for Kyoto to go to school. There's no way of knowing now what kind of beauty he believed in, but as he pondered his own heritage, he said he understood you, father. He was intrigued by the fact that you deserted the army and he respected you for that. He was also filled with uncertainty about whether you and mother were really in love with each other. On the one hand, it seems that he was constantly yearning for some Grecian clarity, but on the other hand, it may be that he did not believe in anything. At this point it is not even clear whether or not he was in love with Shizuko. He only believed in the impulse to love. I have felt that that was the only thing he could immerse himself in. While he was in Kyoto, all he did was go around to see Nō plays. I understand that grandfather had built the Nō at his house in Kamakura as early as 1933. I have no idea when Tarō became interested in the Nō, but he did talk to grandfather about it. While he was in middle school, he spent all his time playing the piano, so I expect he discovered the Nō after he went to Kyoto. He often talked to me about music, but never about the Nō. Among the four of us grandchildren—Kenkichi, Shizuko, Tarō, and me, I think grandfather liked Tarō best. Grandfather's interest in the Nō was nothing more than that of a dilettante, but Tarō apparently discovered that the Nō could be ranked with Greek tragedy. He was constantly searching for something steadfast and unchanging. In the Nō there is an unmasked style of performing. It is a style of Nō that can be danced without wearing a mask. Nō actors, after they pass the age of forty, no longer have their youthful beauty, so they cannot perform this unmasked style. Actors use this style because even if one's art is good, one cannot otherwise display one's youthful beauty. By the time he was twenty, Tarō was already wearing masks. No, I think he was wearing masks in his daily life

long before that. He kept everything hidden behind a
mask. Without understanding this, we will not understand that he kept aloof from the war, and that at the age
of twenty could already foresee his own death. We cannot understand that he destroyed himself with all the in-
tegrity and violence of his own being. It was this aspect
of Tarō that grandfather had loved so much."

"You say he was a bright boy; I remember that much
about him," said Yi. The white lighthouse glittered in the
September sunlight, and on Sagami Bay the whitecaps
were whipped up by the wind.

"Tarō and I talked to Shizuko and then quietly packed
our things. That was on the evening of the fifteenth.
After we had gotten tickets from Uncle Kyŏng-myŏng,
we stopped at a moving company at Kurihama on the
way home and made arrangements for them to pick up
our things the following day. Tarō told Shizuko to bring
nothing more than a single change of clothes. That night
Tarō talked about Mozart for a while and then went to
bed. The next morning we went to grandfather and informed him that we planned to go to Kyoto and take Shizuko with us. Grandfather said nothing, but gazed out
the window at Sagami Bay spread out below."

Jirō's thoughts went back to that time — the gray
lighthouse bathed in the August morning light, the
sound of the surf breaking on the shore, and the asters
blooming in profusion in the garden.

Yasumasa gazed fixedly at the world outside and did
not move. The fresh morning breeze brought the smell

of the beach into the room.

"You have taken care of us for so long, grandfather, that it is a hard thing for us to tell you that this day has finally come. Kenkichi is the head of the Iwami family, and what he is asking of us is only natural. The only question," said Tarō, "is whether we leave now or later. Kenkichi's father was killed in action while our father deserted from the army, and as a consequence the Iwami family has fallen on hard times. This has angered Kenkichi. I don't know what lies ahead, but I expect that after I graduate from Kyoto University, even I will become a normal member of Japanese society. Please wait for that time to come."

There was silence for a time. The brothers stared at the back of their grandfather who gazed fixedly out the window without moving.

"Do you have anything to say, Jirō?" asked Yasumasa, breaking the silence.

"I have nothing to add to what Tarō has already said. Of course I feel that I would like to come back and go fishing soon."

Grandfather was weeping. No matter what we might have said, no argument would have overcome his silence; in that moment we all understood each other's feelings. Grandfather's heart must have been filled with thoughts of the past and of the present, the past and the future—of his own sister who was in Korea, of his nephews born of that sister and a Korean, of that nephew who had married Yasumasa's daughter, of the two boys who had been born to them, of the boys' father who had deserted the army, of his daughter who had to leave those children behind and marry into a different family, of his son who had been killed in the war, of his granddaughter who was about to be taken away to Kyoto—all these things. He did not want us to see him weeping; so he remained the whole time gazing out the window. Presently he spoke, still keeping his back to us, saying, "I have gotten some money together for you. I saw you packing your things last night, but I felt it would do no good to try and stop you. The only thing I hope for is that when you finish school, you will come back and live near here." At this time both Tarō and I felt very strongly each of the sad partings that grandfather had experienced. After that we left grandfather's room and waited for the movers to come. We decided to leave Tsurugigasaki around noon. Even though we were taking the night train, we had to get in line early at Tokyo Station in order to get seats. No one had seen Kenkichi that morning and everyone wondered where he was. There was no trace of his uniform, his black shirt, his bamboo spear, or of the shoes he usually wore; so his mother said she supposed he had gone to the Dawn Society branch headquarters in Yokosuka. We found out later that Kenkichi was hiding in his closet all this time. It was about eleven o'clock when the movers came for the luggage. After that we all gathered at the table for lunch, and grandfather, grandmother, and Aunt Haruko all wished us a safe trip. Shortly after noon we left the house taking Shizuko with us. Since the end of the war had been announced the previous day, there were no attacks by carrier based planes, and even when they did come over, it was only for reconnaissance. It was a quiet moment. The only sound was that of the ocean. Grandfather and Aunt Haruko decided to go with us as far as Matsuwa, so we set out. At that moment Kenkichi appeared in the front garden.

The sunlight was shooting down from straight overhead; Kenkichi was wearing his black-shirted uniform and army helmet. He grasped his bamboo spear in his right hand and sweat stood out on his face.

"You cannot take Shizuko with you," he said.

It was a ghastly voice. The war was over, there were no enemy planes overhead; it was strangely silent at high noon and the only sound was the regular pulsing of the sea. Kenkichi's voice echoed loudly in this stillness. Grandfather stepped forward and scolded him, "Kenkichi! What is the meaning of this?" We could sense in grandfather's voice an anger we had never known before. Kenkichi returned the abuse saying, "Whose side are you on? The Koreans' or the Japanese'?" At that moment Tarō pulled grandfather back and placed himself between Kenkichi and the rest of us.

"Kenkichi, you cannot keep Shizuko and me from going."

"I said I was going to kill you."

"That's right. I heard you say that. And you heard my reply."

"You filthy Korean! It was all on account of you Koreans that we Japanese were defeated. Your father was a filthy Korean and a traitor to Japan. You Koreans did not cooperate with us. You're the kind of dog that bites his master. You son of a bitch! Do you think I will let you go on and stain the purity of a Japanese woman?"

"Stand back, Kenkichi! No one can stop Shizuko and me."

Tarō held Shizuko's left hand in his right; he held their traveling bag in his left hand. He walked toward Kenkichi.

"Let go of Shizuko's hand, you son of a bitch! Let go of my sister's hand."

I think they must have been about twenty feet apart. Tarō held Shizuko's hand and walked slowly, straight at Kenkichi. At that moment Kenkichi made his move. With a strange cry he leveled his bamboo spear and lunged at Tarō. The spear struck Tarō in the stomach. He did not try to get out of the way. Kenkichi withdrew the spear and jabbed again as Tarō began to crumple forward. The spear penetrated the left side of his throat, this time Tarō fell forward as Kenkichi withdrew the spear. As Shizuko and I took Tarō in our arms, he smiled coldly. Kenkichi was shouting and swearing, "Ask for mercy, you damned Korean. Beg for mercy!" When grandfather took the spear and pointed it at Kenkichi, he fled from the garden still screaming wildly.

"The stupid fool! He really did use the spear after all. The poor fellow, let him be. I am going to die a little sooner than I expected, but now that it's come to this, my short life of twenty years has been a long one. I feel as though I have lived for forty years. Remember Jirō, the only thing a person of mixed blood can believe in is beauty. It's a sin to have mixed blood. No one can save you from that sin. Say good-bye to mother for me."

Tarō was gasping for breath and smiling coldly. The ground was stained with the blood that gushed from his throat. The sun was straight overhead and we were drenched in sunlight; a midsummer sea breeze was blowing.

"He killed one of his own blood relatives!" Shizuko was smeared with blood, "Tarō!" she screamed and fainted holding Tarō's head on her knees.

Tarō's carotid artery had been severed by the spear. I stared at the blood gushing from his throat and felt dizzy. I thought, 'This is mixed blood, it was because of this blood that Tarō was killed.' I began to feel angry. It was not anger at Kenkichi, or at Japanese society, rather it was anger at myself and my own mixed blood. It was more than an hour later that the doctor and the police arrived. Kenkichi had gone to the Korean ghetto in Misaki to kill the Koreans who were said to have caused disturbances there the previous day. Actually, the Koreans were celebrating their independence. Kenkichi was arrested there, but on the way to the police station he overpowered the guard and fled. His whereabouts were unknown until the spring of 1949. It was Kenkichi's Japanese blood that made him kill Tarō. By the same token, Tarō knew that he was going to die; it was his Korean blood that made him take Shizuko's hand and advance toward Kenkichi. I think it is also possible that Tarō advanced toward Kenkichi thinking, 'He is my blood cousin, he won't attack me; it's just possible he won't attack me.' As this was happening, Tarō was seeing Kenkichi through his Japanese blood. Even though he said that beauty was the only thing he could believe in, I think that deep in his heart, he really believed in human nature.

That night Shizuko threw herself off the cliff. All through the afternoon she had raved deliriously, 'I had only known him so briefly. He killed his own blood relative. I will go with him. God! Now that he has been taken from me, how can I possibly find happiness? My own brother took him from me, but I will follow after him. That's all I can do.' These were the kinds of things she was saying. I was worried about her in this condition and in the middle of the night went to her room to see if she was all right. She was not in her room and the bedding was scattered around. Suddenly I remembered the cliff and roused the rest of the family. The kitchen door was unlocked. I grabbed a flashlight and ran to the cliff. At the edge of the precipice I discovered her clogs and suddenly remembered that her bedding had been cold. I realized it was too late. There was a full tide that night and I was afraid that when the tide went out, her body would be swept out to sea. After I ran to the lighthouse and asked them to call the police at Misaki, I went to the home of Aoki, the fisherman who had been my friend at elementary school, and got him to take his boat out. It was nearly dawn and the fishing boats were just setting out, so all of them searched for Shizuko's body. Still, it was evening before we found her. It was just off Jōgashima. The body had been mutilated by fish and was swollen by the water.

Both grandmother and Aunt Haruko were exhausted and stayed in bed. As I gazed at the white cliffs of Tsuru-gigasaki from the fishing boat at sea, I had a premonition of my own death. It was unbelievable that in the space of one day I had lost both my cousin and my brother. I

thought about both father and mother. It was a moment
when I felt like being swallowed up by the ocean. Tarō
had taken Shizuko's hand and walked forward toward
his own death. He walked forward knowing he would
die; was there no ambivalence in his heart at that moment? At the time I could not understand what made
him do it; I tried to think it was that beauty he believed
in that caused him to destroy himself. He went into sci-
entific research saying it would be disgusting to be sent
off to war and die in a ditch somewhere, and yet, on the
day after the war ended, on the very day he no longer
had to worry about being hit by a bullet, he chose the
path of his own destruction. Gazing up at the white cliffs
of Tsurugigasaki, I kept telling myself that it would be
wrong for me to die. By the time we had retrieved Shizuko's body off Jōgashima and returned to shore, grandfather had gotten Tarō's body released from the hospital.
That night Uncle Kyŏng-myŏng arrived from the Navy
Base and attended the all night vigil. After I had explained what happened, he patted me on the shoulder
and told me that since I was the only one left, I would
have to be strong. At dawn he went into the forest and
shot himself. I was exhausted and had dozed off when I
heard the pistol shot. I knew Uncle Kyŏng-myŏng had a
pistol, so I looked around to see if he was still in the
room where we were keeping vigil. The people there
said the gunshot had come from the forest, and they
wondered what it was this time. At that moment I suddenly realized it was suicide. Perhaps my own mind was
obsessed with death, since in one day's time I had lost
two people who were close to me and had had a premo-

nition of my own death. Uncle Kyŏng-myŏng had sat down crossed-legged with his back to the trunk of a large Keyaki tree and shot himself in the forehead. He left a last testament and a large sum of money. This was his testament:

"I am sorry to have chosen this place to die; please forgive me. This was the only place in Japan I could come back to. I would be grateful if you would bury me beside Tarō. The money is part of my wages. Please send it to the bereaved families of those many Korean cadets of mine who have been scattered over the south seas. I have attached to this a list of their names and addresses in Korea.

Jirō, please be strong and live. You will probably think me a coward, but there is no other choice left to me now that Japan has been defeated."

"Father, you deserted the army to become a Korean. He, on the other hand, tried to become a Japanese. Japan's defeat repudiated that attempt and he could not return to Korea, so he chose to take his own life. This is the only way to interpret his suicide. Also, perhaps he felt discriminated against because of his brother who deserted the Japanese Army. Even in the Navy he always seemed to be walking under a shadow. Three lieutenant commanders who shared quarters with him and a number of lower ranking people came and politely offered incense at the altar. When the funerals for the three of them were over, all I could feel was desolation in my heart. From that time on grandmother and Aunt Haruko stayed in bed every day and grandfather never left his room. It took all my endurance just to get through each day. I thought about the sympathy Tarō had always had for mother during his lifetime, and I asked grandfather not to let mother see Tarō's body. I informed mother only after the body had been buried. Those three days were a terrible nightmare—everywhere, the smell of blood. So all I have are these gloomy memories and I never came back to visit these graves until last month."

In front of the lighthouse before them they could hear the voices of a group of young men and women who had apparently just gotten off the bus.

"It was never as peaceful as this. Everything was gray; all we could see was the sea and the sky, airplanes and soldiers and damaged ships being towed into the Yokosuka Navy Yard."

"What happened to Kenkichi?" asked Yi. As he spoke, he took his brother's testament which Jirō had handed him and returned it to its envelope.

"In the spring of 1949, he returned like a ghost to Kamakura. It was a Sunday afternoon in early April when they were performing Nō chants in the Nō pavilion. Grandmother had died of a heart attack in 1946. The following year Aunt Haruko died of pneumonia and grandfather spent all his time in the Nō pavilion reading old books. His store in Nihonbashi had been dealing mainly in imported silk, but in those days there was no merchandise available to reopen the store, so he was very discouraged and never left the house. Fortunately, the store itself had not burned and was still standing, but grandfather sold it. He probably realized that I had no intention of becoming a businessman. His only consolation was to get together with his friends who practiced Nō chants and spend half a day with them. I remember that afternoon very clearly. One old woman had arrived late and I escorted her up the hill to the Nō pavilion. As I came back down I saw a gaunt-looking man standing in the garden. He was standing under a cherry tree in full bloom, gazing up at the flower-filled sky. 'Aren't you Kenkichi?' I called out without thinking. He turned to me, 'Jirō?' There was a moment of silence and then he asked, 'Is Tarō here?' I noticed that his eyes were not focused and I had a premonition of the worst. 'Kenkichi,' I said, 'Tarō is no longer alive.' 'That's what I thought,' he said with tears in his eyes. The following day we had him committed to the Kamakura Mental Institute, and when he died half a year later, he was wasted away to skin and bone. He took no nourishment at all. Because he died, I never learned what had happened during the years and months he had been gone. Shortly after Kenkichi had run away, Aunt Haruko often wept, saying he had not been like this when he was a child. On that spring day he was exhausted from his wandering, he no longer re-membered what had happened to him. I expect he had returned to Tsurugigasaki to see his cousin whom he himself had killed. Indeed, he probably went back to Tsurugigasaki before he came to Kamakura. He had a miserable life."

When he finished speaking, Jirō felt as though the feel-ings he had had in his heart for seventeen years had sub-sided.

"It is just as your grandfather said earlier, all that is left is to try to understand. After all these years and months we can do nothing but try to understand. Thank you for telling me all this. Let's go take a look at the place where you two did so much fishing. There is just one more thing; may I keep this testament?"

"You may have it. I think Uncle Kyŏng-myŏng would want you to have it."

Presently they made their way through the asters and down the slope. The sun was setting and the black pines cast long shadows.

When they had gone down the slope of Tsurugigasaki and through the ravine, the beach appeared as though the tide had just receded and the rocky shore was still wet. On the rocks where they had so often sat with their simple, old-fashioned fishing poles were a number of men now fishing with modern reels. Beyond the swirling current, Bōsō was shrouded in haze and in the other direction, beyond Sagami Bay, they could see just the peak of Ōshima Island. The sea wind was blowing and the white-capped waves were breaking on the rocky shore just as they had seventeen years earlier. Gazing at this scene that had remained so completely unchanged, Jirō felt the gloomy landscape that had been scorched on his heart gradually dissolve.

5

"I don't have time to go back to Kamakura, so please give your grandfather my regards. I will come again on my way back from America," said Yi when the car started back from Tsurugigasaki.

"There is something I have been wanting to ask you, father. Haven't you ever felt any uncertainty on account of your mixed blood?" As he spoke, Jirō looked out the window at the line of low mountains on the Miura Peninsula.

"That's a hard question—I've had some uncertainties. I expect I have experienced these uncertainties a good deal more than you have. After all, you boys have mostly Japanese blood and from the time you were children you have been raised as Japanese. That was not the case with me. When you speak of being caught in the middle, no one has experienced this more clearly than my brother and me. Of course there were a certain number of pure Koreans who were at the Japanese military academies and who hoped to become soldiers, so it was a natural thing for my brother and me that, having mixed blood, we should want to become soldiers when our father insisted on it. But it was during the time I spent at the academy that I learned that to live as a Japanese is too restrictive. Have you ever heard the name Kita Ikki?"

"Yes. I know something about him."

"I see. Do you also know the name Nishida Zei?"

"Yes."

"Let me explain briefly. While I was at the military academy I went with a Chinese classmate to meet Nishida. He was in the thirty-fourth class at the academy and was assigned to the Hiroshima Division, but he fell ill and withdrew from the army. It was this Nishida who introduced me to Kita Ikki. That was in the autumn of

1926. Before that, at Nishida's urging I had read several books by Kita. I was especially impressed by one part called 'Revised Policy for the Present and Future Occupation of Korea and Other Areas.' For me, to live as a Japanese was to live in a limited world, but there were no restraints to living as a Korean. There were many unexplored worlds stretching out before me. Tarō had already been born, but when I thought about the future of my children, I decided to register them as members of Hisako's family. I had one more reason for deciding to live my life as a Korean. It is a matter of human goodness. A while ago you spoke of a person being both an oppressor and an oppressed person; I chose to side with the oppressed. I made this decision on the basis of reason, not sentimentality. I was taken by Nishida to Sendagaya to the home of a man named Yamamoto. That is where Kita was living. He was like a kind of patriarch and there were a lot of young officers going in an out of the place. He was an attractive young man – he could have been an actor. I met Kita on two more occasions. The last time was in the summer of 1927; at that time he had moved to Ushigome Nandocho. By that time I was no longer interested in Kita's political faction. It was a group that spent its time arguing against democracy and socialism and anarchism. We can probably say that they were fascists without any theoretical principles, they were acting without any theory. In one sense Kita was a bully, but he was also very cunning. Still, his one statement concerning Korea stayed with me. It was a statement I could not have accepted if I had been pure Korean, but as it was, I could accept it. My mixed blood made it possible. For that reason I was not very well liked by Koreans at that time. Right after I broke with Kita, I took my family and returned to Taegu on assignment. Shortly afterward I was ordered back to the war college and I returned alone to Japan. From Kamakura I commuted to the college, which in those days was in Aoyama Kitamachi. After a while I brought the family to Japan, but as soon as I graduated, we returned to Taegu. From then until the outbreak of the North China Incident was the happiest time for you children and your mother. During that period, I changed. Despite the uncertainty I felt about having mixed blood, I was sustained by the thought that I was on the side of the oppressed. Still, I did not become a Communist. If I had become a Communist, I think I would have deserted the army much sooner. The outbreak of the war forced me to make a decision. I had no way of seeing the future, but when I considered what had happened since the Manchurian Incident and the Shanghai Incident, I realized that it would be a long war and for that reason Japan would probably lose. I talked with some of the Korean officers who said that if that happened, Korea had a chance of gaining her independence. So I deserted the army. Three months later I went to America. What I experienced during the war is beyond imagining. In 1941 when Japan attacked Pearl Harbor, I was convinced that Korea would achieve independence. I began working as a Korean and have not changed since. At some point during my youth I abandoned my uncertainties. That is all I can tell you. How about you, do you feel certain now that you have become Japanese?"

"I am ninety percent sure. The ten percent uncertainty is there because I am not always accepted by the Japanese."

"What do you mean?"

"The idea that art and scholarship know no boundaries is a foreign idea. This may not be clear to you, father, since you have only half Japanese blood, but it represents an island mentality. It is this that keeps me from being accepted. When people ask, I reply that I have some percentage of Korean blood. When they hear this, their attitudes change instantly. They become cold and indifferent. The Japanese people are unique. I think foreigners cannot understand this unreasonable faith in the Emporer. But whether they accept me or not is a separate question; I have no choice but to live as a Japanese. Grandfather often tells me I am unnecessarily concerned about this idea of mine. Also, this, too, is a separate problem, but my two children are completely Japanese. Without realizing they have some percentage of Korean blood themselves, they talk about others and say, 'Oh, he's a Korean.' They learn these attitudes from the older generation of Japanese. But I think it is in evitable since they were born into this unusual Japanese environment."

"We have no choice but to try and understand, I have no choice but to try and understand my brother who joined the Japanese Navy and ended up committing suicide. Let me explain my present situation. Although it does not seem likely, there could possibly some day be a war between Japan and Korea. If that were to happen, I as a Korean soldier would do everything I could to de-

stroy Japan, my mother's country. Your children, on the
other hand, would be killing Koreans. That's the way
history is. I cannot bring myself to make the paradoxical
statement that this is a vicious and eternal circle. If there
is a gulf between us, then so be it. I was seized by a fear
that I would not be able to understand you, but now I
feel that to some extent I have been able to. What about
you?"

"Yes, I think that you and I have no choice but to follow our own separate destinies. In my imagination I did
not feel that I was separated from you, father, but in fact
we really are separated. But I guess that is inevitable. I
am grateful just for the fact that we have been able to
meet."

"We'll probably be able to meet again."

Jirō got out of the car in front of Yokosuka Station. Yi
went on to Yokohama and Tokyo.

6

Yi's return to Japan on his way back from America was
later than he had planned. It was in the middle of January.

Shortly after nine o'clock one evening Jirō received a
telephone call from his father. He explained that he
would be leaving from Haneda International Airport the
following evening, that he would be occupied with business during the day, and that in the evening he would at-

tend a reunion of classmates from the Army Academy that had been planned since September, so he would not be able to come to Kamakura. Jirō asked where the reunion was being held. It was to be from four until six o'clock at a certain Chinese restaurant in Hibiya. Jirō conveyed this information to his grandfather and Jirō decided to go to the reunion.

When he had met his father in September, they had not talked about his mother, Hisako. Even though a long time had passed since his parents had separated, something of the experience remained inside Jirō and would not go away. Early in October he had gone to visit his mother and told her of his father's visit.

"I read about it in the newspapers. What did you talk about with him?"

"Father did not say anything at all about his own life in Korea. We did not talk about you either. But of course I —" Jirō spoke of his undiminished feeling for both his parents. He urged her, if possible, to meet Yi when he returned to Japan from the United States.

"I am not so sure, but if you think it is a good idea, perhaps I will."

Hisako must have been about fifty-five or fifty-six years old. She had a son and a daughter after she married into the Shinjō family. They were both university students now and the boy was attending the university where Jirō taught. She was still very beautiful for a woman who had borne four children. Jirō , having lived away from her since he was sixteen, sometimes felt dazzled when he occasionally met her.

On the day his father telephoned, Jirō realized that the

following day would be the only opportunity for his father and mother to meet. He immediately called his mother. He arranged to meet her on the platform of Ōfuna Station at three the next afternoon. But at ten o'clock the next morning his mother called, asking him to go alone.

"Why?"

"I don't think it would accomplish anything for me to meet your father now. I understand this feeling you said you have about your parents, but your father has his own life over there, and I, too, have changed. It would not accomplish anything for us to see how much we both have changed."

"I see. Well, then, all right."

'She may be right,' thought Jirō. 'Maybe father feels the same way; maybe that is why he said nothing about his wife.'

"What time will he be leaving Haneda?"

"Eight o'clock."

"Please say 'hello' to him for me. Even if we met, it would just bring back old memories, and I would surely end up crying. It is better if I do not meet him."

"I understand."

It was a case where the parents lived their own lives and the children had to live their own lives. Thinking about this, Jirō felt rather forlorn.

There were fourteen of Yi's classmates gathered at the Chinese restaurant in Hibiya. Some had died in the war, and some were too far away to be able to come, and in the end it was remarkable that they had gotten this many together. This is what Yi said when he saw Jirō.

He was wearing his Korean Army uniform. Among the guests was one wearing the uniform of a high ranking officer in the Japanese Self-Defense Forces.

Jirō did not pay much attention to what they were saying. He felt he would not have the opportunity to meet his father again; he could only regard this man as a Korean soldier. There was clearly a gap between himself and his father. This was something he had been thinking about since September, but he could think of no way to bridge the gap. It was not the result of having lived apart for so long, it was because his father had become a Korean. The gentleness he had received from his Uncle Kyŏng-myŏng was lacking in his father. There was the coldness here one finds in a general who commands his country's army.

After the reunion, Jirō took a car to Haneda Airport. Yi was already there when he arrived. His father took him aside and said good-bye.

"After I return to Korea, I will be leaving right away for Europe. I will not be visiting Japan again. I do not know yet what significance it has that I have been able to see you and your grandfather again, but now there is nothing for us to do but go our own ways. I will not have a chance to see you again. I do not know much about art and literature, but I do have a feeling that you have more determination than Tarō. Is there anything more you want to say?"

"I am grateful just for the fact that we had a chance to meet again. There is something—In our talks together, you have never said anything about mother."

"I met her here at the airport just a few moments ago.

She is just over there, so you can return to Kamakura together. I have become a stranger to you and perhaps Hisako has become a stranger, too, but at least you live close to one another. You probably feel something in common. Take care of her. One last thing – as a soldier, I am an egoist. At least as far as you people are concerned. You have not asked why I did not get in touch with you sooner, so I will not answer. I am Korean, you are Japanese; this is a distinction we must preserve even though we are related by blood. You spoke earlier about environment and the island mentality of the Japanese; but you must become one of these Japanese, just as I have become a Korean. Please give my regards to your grandfather. Take care of yourself."

With that, Yi strode away to a room reserved for Korean dignitaries. As he departed, Jirō gazed at this father's broad shoulders; he wondered why his father would not let anyone intrude into his personal world. Perhaps that was not his nature, perhaps it was because he was a Korean soldier. Whichever the case, it was not easy to understand. At this moment the feeling that dominated Jirō's heart was one of infinite, desolate loneliness.

After seeing Yi board the plane, Jirō accompanied his mother out of the airport. In the car on the way to Kamata, he asked Hisako if his father had said anything to her.

"No – He asked me to take care of myself."

"What about you?"

"I said nothing to him. Of course I thought it was good to see him, that's why I came."

"Do you have any regrets?"

"None. As a soldier he could not ask my forgiveness
for anything he had done. I am the one who felt that I
should come and meet him. When he told me to take
care of myself, I felt I had forgiven him."

"I see. It has certainly taken a long time, hasn't it."

"It feels as though it were just yesterday. Your father
has always been able to get a woman flustered and
worked up, while he can go off and leave them without
turning a hair. Well, that's enough of this kind of talk.
How are your children getting along?"

"They're both doing just fine." As he replied Jirō felt
that he was seeing an aspect of his mother he had not
known. He wondered if she still loved his father.
Hisako's attitude could be interpreted that way as well.

7

Three weeks after he had seen his father off, Jirō and
Yasumasa went again to visit Tsurugigasaki. "I won't be
around much longer and I have been thinking about
moving these three from Tsurugigasaki to the Iwami
family plot in Kamakura." As Yasumasa grew older, his
heart grew fonder of those who had died. "Anyway, let's
go take a look at the graves," said Yasumasa. For his part,
Jirō felt as though he would be able to resolve his gloomy
feelings about Tsurugigasaki because he had had a
chance to meet his father again. In a sense, Jirō was
redeemed by what his father had said at the airport: "I

am Korean, you are Japanese; this is a distinction we must preserve even though we are related by blood." Jirō felt that now more than ever he could understand Yi. His father said that he had had some concern over having mixed blood, but that he had lost that somewhere during his youth, and Jirō did not disbelieve him. With the passage of time he came to see very clearly the unmoving image of a soldier who had sworn his allegiance to Korea. As a student of pure Japanese literature, Jirō had not been the object of prejudice in post-war Japanese society. In a sense he was fortunate that his fellow students and colleagues were all good natured. The fact that his brother had been stabbed to death by his own relative, his cousin had killed herself to follow him in death, and his uncle had committed suicide—all these things were a tragedy born of mixed blood, and this still disturbed Jirō. After the nightmare experience of those three days, he remembered that he had been obsessed with the feeling that he could always smell blood around him.

A strong wind was blowing at Tsurugigasaki. The white lighthouse stood out vividly beneath the pale winter sun. The function of the lighthouse was simply to light up the sea at fixed intervals. Jirō felt as though he had discovered in this pattern something eternal that he had lost sight of.

Yasumasa looked at the three gravestones that had been erected among the wind-whipped stems of the now withered asters. His grandfather's figure was much like one of those withered stems. Jirō thought about the seasons to come when the asters would bloom luxuriantly in whites and reds and crimson.

"I wonder if it would be a good idea to move Tarō next to Kenkichi," said Yasumasa.

"I think so. Tarō always had an air of futility about him. Just before he died he forgave Kenkichi." Recalling the ghostly figure of Kenkichi when he returned to Kamakura seeking the Tarō he himself had killed, Jirō felt that only when he had gone insane could Kenkichi accept others with compassion, as human beings. Jirō recalled how he had looked up at the sky through the fully opened cherry blossoms and asked tearfully, "Is Tarō here?" It showed that there was a bond linking Kenkichi and Tarō and Jirō. It was the Japanese blood in Kenkichi that had stabbed Tarō and it was also Kenkichi's Japanese blood that had brought him back in search of the Tarō he had killed.

"In the case of Uncle Kyŏng-myŏng's grave, it is all right that it be without a posthumous name."

"It is as you requested, grandfather."

"I see. Compared to Yi who had iron in his soul, this man who killed himself as a Japanese soldier is in fact a Japanese. The Koreans will condemn him and the Japanese will forget him, but we can understand his feelings."

If it is true as Tarō said that having mixed blood is a sin, then Uncle Kyŏng-myŏng endured that stigma alone and the only choice he had open to him when Japan was defeated was to commit suicide. That is how Jirō felt.

"Did you accomplish anything at all by meeting your father?"

"Father said, 'Even though we are related by blood, we must maintain the distinction between Japanese and Korean.'"

"How did you interpret that?"

"It made me realize that the world is very harsh. But, of course, I thought that was the correct way to live."

"When shall we move the graves? We should probably do it on the anniversary of their death."

"Yes, I think that would be good." Jirō looked up at the hard, clear winter sky and realized at that moment what a long road he had traveled. Those dark summer shadows from just after the end of the war were now, he felt, dispelled. He and Tarō had faced uncertainty and agony, but their experience had probably been minor compared to that of their father. Now at last Jirō believed that he had transcended his destiny.

THE ARCHER

1

The Shinto celebration known as Yabusame is a form of equestrian archery in which men shoot arrows at targets from galloping horses. Tradition has it that the celebration began in the Heian period and flourished in the Kamakura and Momoyama periods.* Masako could not imagine how it evolved into the formal ritual of today's Yabusame and came to remain in various places as one of the regular Shinto observances celebrated during the course of the year.

Five years earlier Masako had married at the age of twenty-five. Her husband, Takehiko Kitō, had already retired from horseback riding and archery, and in his place his younger brother, Takeji, participated in the Yabusame celebration at the Hachiman Shrine in Kamakura each year. There was a difference of nine years in the ages of the brothers, and Takeji, just twenty-one, was indeed a handsome youth. Masako's first impression of him could be summed up in the single word "dignity." Takeji wore the old courtly hunting costume, a woven red hat, and carried a Shigetō bow* in his gloved hands. On his galloping horse he was a figure of masculine dignity of a sort Masako had never encountered while growing up.

The targets were squares of wood hung on fresh bamboo twigs. That year Takeji displayed his virtuosity by shattering all three targets with his arrows. Takehiko, standing on the sidelines, said that to hit the mark three times was no easy task.

"When did he learn to shoot like that? I get the feeling he's the one who inherited my father's blood, not me."

"Surely you must have scored three hits many times in your career," suggested Masako glancing up at her husband's profile.

"No. I could never train my body that hard. Hitting it twice was all I could ever manage. I would hit the first target, quickly pull an arrow from my quiver and fit it to the bow, but by then I had already passed the second target and was coming up on the third. Takeji's always been a frail boy, but he practiced hard for this. Well, I've got other things to think about."

"What do you mean?"

"Nothing. It has nothing to do with you, it's a business matter."

Two years after that her husband, Takehiko, bought the contract of a Yanagibashi geisha and set her up in a house at Gōtokuji in Setagaya and gave her the money she needed to open a small restaurant. After that he no longer returned to his home in Kamakura.

Meanwhile, Takeji had developed into a young man with rare skill as a rider in the Yabusame performance. Since he loved archery and horseback riding, it was no struggle for him to develop his skill. Nevertheless, to hit a target at thirty meters from a galloping horse is unusual. It is not surprising then that he demonstrated his preeminent skill at the Yabusame festival where the targets were only two arrow lengths away.

For generations the Kitō family had adopted the notion that children must be raised strictly. In this respect Takeji and Takehiko's mother, Shizuka, was a wise woman. She did not allow her children to cry or fuss. She limited the maids' duties to working in the kitchen; everything from cleaning the garden to cutting firewood to heat the bath was assigned to Takeji. She even made her two married daughters wash their own underwear when they were at home.

For this reason Takeji, who worked in an architectural firm, had the task every morning of sweeping and watering the path from the front door to the gate and part of the street beyond. Another chore he never failed to do was cleaning the barn. While other youths owned cars, Takeji's one extravagance was to own a single, fine horse that was crippled.

This year the Yabusame festival was to be held on September sixteenth. Takeji had formally entered the competition and never seemed to question the nature of this ritual performance. As Masako watched, she had the impression that all the ritual and the restrictions of the ceremony were a way he had of disciplining himself.

At one point Masako's mother-in-law Shizuka spoke to her saying, "That boy has always been a weakling, but he demands a lot of himself and has trained too hard. Sometimes I feared for his health."

Masako had seen this in Takeji all along, but ever

since her husband had left home three years before, she felt as though the image she had of Takeji was that of perfect youth. Although she tried to deny its existence, she could not. She tried to persuade herself that this was not really Takeji who occupied her thoughts, it was an image of ideal youth, but in the end, all this was nothing more than rationalization.

Takeji's horse was a male thoroughbred four-year-old he had bought in Hokkaido three years ago. It seems that half the cost of the horse was put up by his father, Kōichi. Masako had been present and heard Kōichi say, "You needn't pay back the money as long as you keep training with the horse and archery. But if at any time you give it up for no good reason, I will insist that the money be returned along with interest ammounting to three sen per day." No doubt Kōichi was afraid Takeji might turn out to be a playboy like his brother despite the great effort they had taken in raising their children rigorously.

Takeji's horse was called Phoenix. His bloodline had been traced and he had a very good pedigree, but there was one flaw that made him unsuitable as a race horse. His right foreleg was four centimeters shorter than his other three legs. The problem could be corrected by giving him a horseshoe on that foot that was four centimeters thicker than the others, but because of this defect, he could never be a race horse.

Takeji had heard about this horse from his brother's friend, Katsuyuki Tajima, and also at the riding club. Since the price was cheap he became interested and talked the matter over with his father. In the end he bought the horse for an unbelievably low price, had a 2.5 centimeter horseshoe put on the right foreleg, and sent it to be trained. Before long Phoenix could run as well as any other horse.

Masako had observed Takeji throughout this period and saw the image of pure youth in him.

2

At last the busy summer drew to a close. One Sunday afternoon in late August, Masako returned to her family home at Kamakurayama on an errand of some sort. It was past three o'clock when she left there and walked to the bus stop at Takasago. Cherry trees lined the quiet street and sunlight filtering through their leaves dappled the ground. Waiting for the bus, Masako gazed at a solitary spot of brilliant sunlight and let her thoughts drift. Faintly, far in the distance she seemed to hear the sound of hoof beats. The pensive solitude, intensified by the incessant cries of the cicadas, was shattered by the approaching hoof beats.

"Could it be Takeji?" Masako raised her head and looked in the direction of Wakamatsu. The sound of hoofbeats thundered louder and louder as though crossing over from the world of dreams into the world of reality. A moment later she caught sight of the galloping horse.

The young rider was indeed Takeji. He reined up in front of her. Masako looked up at the radiant figure of her brother-in-law on horseback.

"What brings you here today?" asked Takeji wiping the perspiration from his face with a towel.

"I had an errand to do at my parents' house."

"Oh, that's right, you used to live around here." Takeji dismounted.

"I came over here while you and your father were at the archery range." An archery range had been set up on the grounds of the Kitō family estate.

"I don't suppose Takehiko came home last night?"

"No. You know as well as I do he only comes back about once a month, sometimes not even that often." Masako spoke softly and looked down at the ground.

"I guess you're right. I wonder why he behaves that way?"

"He sent some money yesterday so he probably doesn't intend to come home for a while yet."

"You two certainly are an odd couple."

"Takeji, do I look like a fool to you?" Masako looked up, a breeze brought to her the sweaty masculine smell.

"Maybe it would be better if you did look like a fool — By the way, did father or mother talk to you recently?"

"Why no, they haven't said anything special, is there something I should know? Something about me?"

"Well, sooner or later someone is going to have to tell you — But I wouldn't want you to faint right here in the street; I'll tell you when we get home."

"Look, it's all right. I'm not going to faint. Go ahead and tell me, please. I've fainted before; it's all right."

"Okay, I'll tell you. The other woman has had a baby. It happened this spring, but neither father nor I knew about it until well into the summer."

"I see –" Once again Masakao dropped her gaze. Somewhere inside her she had always expected this might happen, but now that it had happened, now that the other woman had actually had a baby, now that the other woman had something she did not have; the thought of it made her feel miserable. This feeling passed through her in a flash and was gone. Masako quickly regained control of herself and asked, "Well, is it a boy or a girl?"

"It's a boy. I'm sorry I had to be the one to tell you this. Please don't hold it against me."

"No. Of course not, that's quite all right. Sometimes it's better to know about things like this right away." Masako sighed and her shoulders slumped as though the spirit had suddenly gone out of her.

"It's been about three years now, hasn't it, since Takehiko left home? It can't have been easy for you to go along like this for three years."

"Are you trying to comfort me?"

"Yes, I guess so – What I mean is, I can't understand why any man would go off and leave a woman like you all alone for three years."

"What do you mean, Takeji?"

"Here comes the bus. Be sure to fix something good for dinner tonight." Takeji mounted his horse and spurred off.

Masako boarded the bus that had finally arrived. The days had long since passed when she thought about her husband who was living with another woman. Without quite being aware of it, she had stopped lying awake at night wondering when her husband would come back. For the last half year or more she felt as though she had been able to go on by simply enduring each day, one day at a time. Her husband had a wild, destructive nature in contrast to his father and brother who were able to live at peace with themselves. Her husband did not have his father's level-headed businessman's nature and she wondered if perhaps that was what had driven him to his present situation. Even now, it seemed, he only showed up about three afternoons a week at the Kitō family store. The family's wholesale fabric store had been operating in Horidome of Nihonbashi for four generations. Her husband was a vice-president in the store's management and each month he sent to Masako the salary he received for that.

The woman at Gōtokuji operated a small restaurant and employed three girls. Takehiko seemed to have the leisure to spend most of each day idling there in his elegant Tōzan kimono drinking sake. Masako's father-in-law only muttered, "He's a fool!" and her mother-in-law Shizuka had tried to comfort her by saying, "He'll come back one of these days." But that was two years ago. Now that a child had been born, however, it was not so easy to suppose that he would come back.

Masako had never been to the house in Gōtokuji and of course she had no idea what sort of person the other woman was. Having heard about the baby from her brother-in-law, something seemed to die within Masako, but at the same time, something quite different began to grow. Masako recalled that Takeji had said he could not understand why any man would go off and leave a woman like her alone for three years. Takeji had a strict sense of character and she felt sure he was not lying to her when he said that. Time passed and still Takeji's words reverberated in her heart, binding it tighter and tighter. 'But what he suggests—it could hever happen.' Masako realized now that she was in a difficult situation.

3

One evening several days later, just as Masako was about to take tea upstairs to Takeji's room, she heard her father-in-law Kōichi's angry voice. Masako stayed at the foot of the stairs listening as Kōichi said, "I want you to go to Gōtokuji and make my intentions perfectly clear to him. And I want you to bring back an answer."

"Wouldn't it be better, father, if you talked directly to him yourself? He shows up at the store sometimes, doesn't he?"

"He always avoids me. I want you to go this Saturday afternoon, all right?"

"It's not going to be a very pleasant chore, but I'll go."

"You get off the train at Gōtokuji. It's right in front of the station. The place is called 'Yayoi no Sato.'* Isn't that just cute? It sound like the kind of name a school girl would use. He says Yayoi was her professional name when she was a geisha. She's an attractive woman, though, any man would see that. But I don't want you to

99

pay any attention to her; just bring back his answer. Maybe you should take Masako with you."

"Masako?"

"It's time we really bring him to his senses."

"Masako won't go. She has too much pride to do something like that."

"Oh, really? – I never thought of her that way, but maybe you're right."

Masako listened until the conversation got this far and then withdrew to another room. After a while it sounded as though Kōichi had come downstairs and presently he went along the corridor to the detached room. Masako hesitated a moment and then went upstairs.

"I overheard your conversation a few minutes ago. I just caught part of it, so I didn't really understand; what is father asking you to do?" Masako placed the tea in front of Takeji as she spoke.

"He's asked me to deliver an ultimatum; either Takehiko returns here or he gives up his position at the store. I'm to bring back his reply." Takeji seemed worried.

"There's no question about it. In that case he will give up the store for sure."

"Why do you say that? Father said that if Takehiko does not come back here, the store will go to his son-in-law, Toyoshiro Sekiguchi. I am sure father would rather not do that. After all, it is a big business; there are five hundred people employed there. Takehiko will come back, father doesn't want to give it to Sekiguchi."

"No, I don't think so. Takehiko once told me that the people who want money or status are the kind who can think of nothing but how to pay their bills. He thinks it is just a waste of time to be an executive and try to tell other people what to do. In that respect, I think he is quite satisfied with the kind of life he can lead at Gōto-kuji."

"Are you prepared to accept that, Masako?"

"If it comes to that, I intend to leave."

"You mean you'll get a divorce?"

"That's right. I'll go back to my parents' home in Kama-kurayama — If that happens, Takeji, will you come visit me sometimes, when you are out riding?"

"Masako, I'm hoping that Takehiko will come back to you — Way back when he first left you, I often had to question myself very carefully about the feelings I had for you. Masako, you've always been close enough so that I could reach out to you. Sometimes it was hard to tell what was real and what was just a fantasy. I had to keep reminding myself that you are my brother's wife even though he has gone to live with another woman. I've spent the whole time up until now trying to be so-cially proper. To be quite honest, I was glad when I real-ized that Takehiko really would not be coming back here. But now, despite that, I hope he will come back to you."

"Why do you hope he will come back to me? Please tell me."

"You're a proud woman, Masako, and you are able to bear a lot. Women like you are very rare these days. At first I thought you didn't even have any jealousy. Yet it seemed inconceivable to me that a woman of your sensi-tivity and depth of emotion could be without feelings in this matter. All your feelings are hidden deep within you. No matter how dissolute and irresponsible my brother becomes, I don't think it likely he will forget a woman like you."

"I understand, Takeji. The fact is that I am really a very jealous woman. But still, if it turns out that I do go back to my parents' home, will you come visit me?"

"I'll come visit you. Once you are divorced from him, I won't have to be ashamed of my feelings for you."

"Don't forget, I'm four years older than you."

"You've been older than I ever since you came to live here. That hasn't changed."

"Yes. Thank you for saying that."

Masako felt it had been a long time since a man had showered her with tender feelings like this. Indeed, this was the very first time a man had spoken to her like this. Her marriage had been arranged by their families. Of course she had had some brief infatuations as a schoolgirl, but today was the first time a man had spoken to her clearly and affectionately like this.

4

When Masako awoke the following Sunday morning, she could hear the twang of a bowstring from the archery range behind the house. After she had put away the bedding and washed her face, she went to the archery range.

The faint morning sunlight, broken by the foliage of

the trees, speckled the damp ground. Just as she came into the shooting range, Takeji, holding the bow in his left hand, drew an arrow from the quiver and fitted it to the string. He drew the string in a certain way. Masako had watched him do this many times and she always felt that it was the moment of utmost tranquility and utmost tension. The bowstring sang. The arrow pierced the September morning light and struck the target, leaving behind only a quivering stillness in the air.

Masako had once heard Takeji say that that instant when he held the bow full drawn and aimed at the target required the same intensity of concentration as trying to walk while carrying a basin full of water.

Among the antiques handed down for many generations in the Kitō family was a Shigetō bow. Takeji said he had not been able to handle that bow until he was sixteen.

"I could only draw it half way. It requires more than just physical strength to draw a bow like that. I'll never forget what happened one morning when I was sixteen. It was a May morning. The sun was not up yet as I stood in the garden still wet with dew. I fitted an arrow to the string and pulling it back all the way, I could see the target over the taut string. When I felt I was ready, I released the arrow. It cut through the air with a crisp sound and hit the target. Up to that time I had not been able to hold the bow completely steady and the arrows had always missed the target. That morning I was truely and fully happy."

Once again Masako saw before her the pure, unblemished figure of Takeji. At regular intervals that perfect

sound came to her ears, the quick snap of an arrow being released, the long hum of the arrow cutting through
the air, the short smack as it hit the target. Again and
again through the summer sunlight, two short sounds
with a long sound between them. This was the pure,
perfect sound of archery.

At that moment Takeji saw nothing but the target. He
thought nothing, felt nothing, but at regular intervals
and with perfect control, he notched the arrows and sent
them humming toward the target. While many of his
schoolmates had been active in the radical student
movement, he had practiced archery by himself. In the
spring of the year he had turned fifteen, he began using
a full-sized bow. He began by shooting at a target fifteen
feet away and increased the distance by five feet each
month. In eight months it was forty feet away, and from
there it had taken a year and a half until he could hit the
target at sixty feet. It took until the summer of his
twenty-fifth year before he could hit the target at one
hundred and fifty feet. He was not satisfied merely to hit
the target, he had to hit the very center of the target. Had
he been a warrior, he would not have been satisfied to
wound his opponent in the arms or legs, he would have
had to pierce the enemy's eye or heart.

"That I am doing this has nothing to do with the fact
that my forefathers were archers. This is something I
sought on my own. When I began learning archery at
the age of twelve, the training first assigned me by my
grandfather seemed rather unusual. He had me just
stand and gaze steadily at the target as I was fitting an arrow to the string and pulling it back. I would stand for

five minutes concentrating on this. Then he had me stand like this for ten minutes. The result of this training was that I could hold the bow and arrow utterly still, my whole body would be perfectly still, and I could see the target just above the bowstring. Then for the first time I had a natural feel for releasing the arrow and hitting the center of the target."

Hearing this story, Masako felt a sense of freshness she had not experienced before. The scene spreading out before her today at the archery range gave her the same feeling.

As Takeji was taking the last arrow from the quiver at his feet, Masako's father-in-law, Kōichi, walked over to her.

"Good morning," said Masako dipping her head in a bow of greeting.

"Isn't this pretty early for you to be up, Masako? Is it time for breakfast already?"

"No. I just now got up. It seems awfully early for him to be practicing so I just came out to watch."

"Just watching, eh? When you make the miso soup this morning, please use some of the Sendai miso."

"Yes. I'll be sure to do that."

As Masako was bowing to Kōichi, she stole a glance at Takeji pulling the bow once more to its full extent. She caught sight of his ancient costume as she withdrew to the house.

Having asked the maid to heat the bath, Masako went into the kitchen. Through the window she saw her mother-in-law walking in the garden looking at the flowers. If only her husband had also been there that morning, her happiness would have been complete. As it was, she had a special feeling of happiness, but along with it was a hurt, a pinprick of regret and uncertainty.

Presently Kōichi came in from the hall and went into the bath. Apparently archery practice was over.

Masako went out the back door into the garden and found Takeji at the stable cutting grass for his horse. "Did you go to Gōtokuji yesterday?" she asked, crouching at the edge of the garden picking lettuce greens for breakfast.

"Yes, I went, but I didn't see Takehiko. The other woman is ill and has been hospitalized. Apparently he was at the hospital."

"Did you see the baby?"

"No. I had to work late yesterday, so I asked the maid to have him call me at my office. He called last night and said he would come here this afternoon."

"I see — I didn't realize you had come back here last night."

"I came back on the last train."

"That must have been an unpleasant encounter for you."

"Oh, it was all right talking to him. For the sake of our family I am hoping that you and Takehiko will get back together again."

"I feel I have to make a choice, but even if he comes back here as you hope, I don't think my life will ever regain what has been destroyed."

"You say you have to make a choice, but it doesn't seem to me that you've ever had a choice in this matter."

"Isn't that only because you don't suppose I have a will of my own in this?"

"I understand. But even if Takehiko does come back here, my feelings for you won't change. You are an old-fashioned woman, and I guess I am just an old-fashioned young man. Don't you think it is good there are people like us in this modern world where everyone else is selfishly looking out for themselves? Mother is coming this way. Please don't scowl like that."

As Takeji spoke, Masako stood up holding her salad greens. She returned to the house by the back door, pausing there to ask, "Will you be home this afternoon?"

"No, I'm going out. As soon as we eat, I'm going for a ride. This afternoon I will go to the Hachiman Shrine to practice for the Yabusame competition."

Masako looked at Takeji and saw that there was nothing to cloud the clearness of his eyes.

It was around noon when Takehiko returned home for the first time in a month and a half. Masako was sitting in the living room reading the newspaper when suddenly a large figure appeared before her and a deep voice rumbled, "Is father here?" Takehiko casually sat down in front of her.

"Both of them are in the detached room," replied Masako lowering her eyes as she folded the newspaper. As she spoke, it occurred to her that Takeji was smart to be out of the house just now. No matter what kind of husband he was, it was natural that she felt guilty about being close to his younger brother during her husband's absence. She was especially conscious of this when her husband was once more there in front of her. She had not expected this feeling.

"I heard you have a child now —"

"Are you being sarcastic?"

"No. I can't have children of my own and I just wondered what the baby is like."

"We named him Satsuki. Since you know about him I feel I should at least tell you his name, but perhaps you think I am just trying to humor you."

"Satsuki? But it's a boy, isn't it?"

"It's an old-fashioned and unfortunate Japanese custom to give boys heroic names. In fact in my own life I've wasted a lot of time because my father is way out of line when it comes to these things. All I've ever wanted to do is write, but he tried to ignore my feelings and force me to study economics. I intend to raise my son properly. But, what have they told you?"

"Well — I've heard a little about it."

"That makes it easier to talk to you about it then. All I have to say to him is that I will not take my position as head of the family. That's all there is to say. I hope you understand my position."

"Then who will inherit the store?"

"He can give it to Takeji. I think my sister Kyoko is trying to maneuver so that her husband, Sekiguchi, can become president of the company, but he'll never make it; I won't let that happen. Takeji's a good fellow; he's pretty conventional, but he's all right."

"Yes, but Takeji has such a scholarly disposition, I wonder if he has any business skill?"

"Business skill? He'll pick that up from the people

around him. As long as there are fools like Sekiguchi around, the Kitō Store will get along. Besides, just because I'm not going to inherit the store does not mean that I am going to quit working there."

"I understand. You mean you won't be coming back here anymore; is that it?"

"That's right. A man rarely encounters a woman like you in this world; I realize that. I think you are an attractive woman. If I were to compare you, for example, to the woman I am living with now, I would say that you are a peony and she is a violet. I like her because she is good and ignorant. What I'm saying is, I find it difficult to be with a flawless woman like you. As a woman you are even more perfect than my own mother. When I married you, I believed imperfection had a certain charm, but afterward I realized my mistake. It's been three years now since I left home. This spring when Satsuki was born, I thought about you, and as you might expect, I felt miserable. I wondered how it was for you living here quietly like this with your husband never around. I wondered what you would do."

"It sounds like you are talking about someone else."

"Yes. But I felt miserable. I even considered talking you into remarrying."

"That's enough. Please go to the detached room."

"I'm sorry for bothering you." Getting lightly to his feet, Takehiko left the room. Staring out at the sunlight through the trees in the garden, Masako listened as her husband's footsteps died away in the direction of the detached room. It occurred to her that those footsteps would never be coming to her again, and of course it hurt her. Their actual married life had lasted less than two years. Somehow he was the kind of man who could leave her here untasted, as it were, and go off with another woman. During those two years they had never really known each other.

A short time later the buzzer rang in the room. Hearing this, the maid appeared, but Masako sent her back saying, "That's all right, I'll go." Responding to Shizuka's summons, she was told, "Takehiko is gone now."

"I see." Masako looked down at her knees and thought about Takeji.

"We were unable to do anything. In this family we have always made allowances for black sheep and renegades and we seem to have produced one in each generation, but he is the worst to come along so far," said Kōichi.

"Talk like this won't help Masako," interrupted Shizuka, "We plan to do all we can for you, but I don't know how we will ever be able to apologize to your parents for this—"

"That's quite all right—Give me a little while to think it over alone, please. After that I will go back to my parents' home." Masako suddenly burst into tears. It was the first time since she had come to the Kitō family that anyone had seen her weep.

At dinner that evening the members of the Kitō family were depressed and quiet, but Masako acted quite normally. She now regretted bursting into tears earlier in the day. It was not that she was overcome with grief at having been abandoned by her husband, or because she had had some bad luck; rather it was a moment of emptiness. Now that everything was over, she felt drained, but she still carried in her heart the image of a simple youth. Masako now felt that her tears had been meaningless.

After dinner Kōichi and Shizuka withdrew to their room and Takeji followed shortly afterwards. They probably wanted to discuss the matter of who would inherit the Kitō store.

After Takeji left the room, Masako waited for some time, but he did not return. She stayed in the living room watching television until after nine o'clock. A short time later the maid came out of the bath and went to her room. The clock struck ten, but Takeji did not return.

5

After the lights went out in the maid's room, Masako waited a while, then went upstairs. There were three rooms on the second floor and Masako softly entered Takeji's den. The room had a musty smell and was littered with architecture magazines and models of houses. The sliding door leading to the adjoining room was open and in the dim light she could see the bedding the maid had laid out earlier. Masako sat down in the desk chair and gazed at the cover of the architecture magazine in front of her.

Presently there were footsteps in the downstairs hall; they ascended the stairs.

"Oh, you're here," Takeji pulled another chair close to Masako and sat down. "I've listened to all the discussions," he said lighting a cigarette.

"I have decided to return to my parents' home at the end of September."

"There is nothing else you can do."

"Are you happy, Takeji, that things turned out this way?"

"My feelings are very complicated and confused, neither joy nor sorrow. How about you?"

"I guess I feel the same way. I feel very tired, empty. When I return to my parents' home, things may go back to normal. I've lived the last three years as though I was dead and I expect it will take a while before I get back to normal — But if you come to see me, I'm sure I'll feel better sooner."

"I'll visit you very soon."

"What about the store? What did you decide about that?"

"We've been talking about that the whole time. I will inherit the store and my brother will stay on to assist until I learn to handle things. That's as far as the discussion went. I agreed to do it with the understanding that I would use part of the building for my architectural offices. I don't intend to give up my work as an architect."

As Masako listened to Takeji talk, she wondered where she fit into all this. If Takeji became head of the family as well, it would mean that she would have to come here once again as a bride. She wondered if something like that could really happen.

"What did my brother say when he talked to you?

Neither mother nor father seemed to know what you
two had talked about—"

"We didn't really talk about anything. He just decided
everything on his own and left. There was nothing I
could do about it. What could I say after waiting three
long years?"

Masako looked down. In the dim light of the desk
lamp she felt as though the blue, unlined kimono she
wore was melting into the room. Something seemed to
flicker in the empty place where her heart belonged.
Masako focused her attention on that something throbbing in her breast. "Takeji." She looked up as she called
his name and quietly stood up. Going into the next
room, she closed the door and standing at the foot of the
bedding, untied her kimono.

6

It was nearly dawn when Masako quietly dressed and
went downstairs. Having returned to her own room and
lain down on her own bed, her breast was filled with
joy, joy at having given herself entirely to an innocent
youth.

Masako retained a clear memory of her first night with
her husband. At that time she had not realized it, but
now after having given herself to an innocent youth, she
knew that on that first night her husband already had
much experience with women. What was this joy that

seemed to gush up inside her body? She pulled up the summer blanket that was already out of season, and feeling a sense of repose she had not experienced in a long time, fell asleep.

In her bed as dawn was breaking, Masako had a dream. In her dream Takeji had buried his face between her breasts.

After that Masako's life began following a new pattern. At eleven o'clock she would go upstairs and at four in the morning return to her own room. When she thought about the past, she felt that she had never known such happiness with her husband. Never having known true joy, her body had begun to atrophy, but now with Takeji she felt it beginning to bloom. This continued for five nights. Masako went about as usual during the day. Her daily activities were no different than usual, but she now felt a sense of repose. On September sixteenth she would see the celebration of the Yabusame and afterwards return to her parents' home. She would wait there expectantly for Takeji's visit. Masako was convinced that there was something between them that would never change.

On the afternoon of the sixth day she went out to do some shopping and returned to find Shizuka waiting for her. Shizuka led her to the detached room and Masako followed. "Come in," said Shizuka looking out at the garden, "Something unexpected has come up; please listen to what I have to say without getting upset. Really, you should be happy about it."

Masako waited uneasily for her mother-in-law's next words wondering if she had found out about her relationship with Takeji or what.

"Takehiko has sent word that he is coming back."

"He is?" Masako broke off, unable to grasp the full meaning of the news.

"The woman at Gōtokuji died. I don't know what was wrong with her, it has some complicated medical name. Once the funeral has been taken care of, he is going to bring the child and come back to live with us. He called shortly after you left to go shopping. I made Takehiko give his promise that he will live here with you for the rest of his life. Of course his father also agreed. Takehiko had already gone to the store to apologize to his father. Masako, you are not able to have a baby of your own. Though it may be difficult, won't you please accept the child as your own and welcome them here? He asked whether or not you had already returned to your parents' house. I think this whole episode of his being at Gōtokuji was just a temporary illusion on his part and I am so happy that you are still here. I feel much better now, Masako." As Shizuka finished speaking she put her hands on her breast and heaved a sigh of relief.

Suddenly Masako saw the bright light of late summer that burned in her heart fade; she was left with an empty feeling of desolation. 'She doesn't know,' thought Masako, 'She thinks I am pleased.' Masako tried to keep calm.

"I don't know what kind of person the woman in Gōtokuji was, but now that she's dead, I feel sorry for her. Still, there is no question that the child is Takehiko's. Of course you can't decide right away, but I do hope you will make up your mind to stay with him." As Shizuka spoke these words, Masako felt that she was getting a glimpse of her own death. It was not that she did not like her husband, and neither did she dislike the idea of the other woman's baby. But her heart was filled with the idea that her life as a woman was ending after only five days.

"Well, when is he coming back?"

"He said it would be the seventeenth or eighteenth. He is selling the shop in Gōtokuji."

Masako thought for a moment and then stood up saying, "Yes, I see." She felt she would faint if she stayed there.

When she got to her room, she looked at her reflection in the mirror. Her face was drained and her eyes seemed to glitter unnaturally. She was no longer concerned with the fact that her husband was being selfish. He had always had a wild and destructive nature.

In the garden, the sun was setting and shadows stretched away in every direction. The Yabusame Festival was to be held on the sixteenth and her husband was due to return the following day. Only two days remained until the Yabusame Festival.

7

That evening Takeji announced that this would be the last year he would ride in the Yabusame Festival.

"You say this will be your last year. Somehow that

sounds like a foreshadowing of what will happen between us."

"It will be better that way, don't you think? Let's not talk any more about my brother coming back, all right? Why don't you listen to me talk about archery instead?"

"I will be happy just listening to anything you have to say."

"I often think about when I was younger. I have already told you how I would fit the arrow to the string and pull with all my might. Grandfather got me started on this unusual way of practicing, but he never forced me to do it. when I think about it now, grandfather was teaching me to conquer myself. As far as I was concerned, it was not just some ancient moral principle in volved. I continued practicing in this unusual way until my arms were so swollen I could no longer hold the bow. As soon as my arms got better, I began practicing again. I feel a great debt of gratitude to my grandfather who raised me this way. Nowdays when we no longer shoot people with arrows, this is no longer a martial art, it is nothing more than a kind of sport, but for me it has become a ceremonial rite. Sports always have some fun and sentimentality to go along with them, but a ritual has only the most severe restraints. To take up my bow and shoot an arrow, that is the world of tranquility. I discovered in this many things about myself, rules for governing my own life. The summer I just turned twenty-five, I used the heavy bow to hit a target dead center at fifty meters; it was then I first felt I could find my own personal freedom within these strict regulations. It was then, for the first time, that I found the ritualized movements of the Yabusame to be more than mere ritual. I no longer cared about the old-fashioned costume or the Shinto celebration; at that moment I gave birth within me to my own personal Yabusame."

"That's interesting. You say you found freedom in regulation?"

"This will be the last year I perform the Yabusame, but I do not intend to give up archery."

They were facing each other across the desk. Masako could feel the dread welling up inside her as she wondered if this meant that everything was finished between them.

"Day after tomorrow in the Yabusame, I plan to use the Shigetō bow that has been handed down in the family for generations. Even though the arrows I use are two pronged, they split the target and go right through the bales of straw set up behind the targets."

"Have you chosen anyone to take your place next year?"

"Yes, Tosa."

"Tosa will be a worthy successor to you, I'm sure."

"He's a good man."

Even though they chatted casually in this fashion, both were aware of the gloom that had settled darkly over them.

8

September sixteenth was a fine, clear day.

Takeji's costume had been laid out the day before. The ancient-style hunting robe had been taken apart, washed, and resewn by Shizuka and Masako several days earlier. As she laid out the other ancient garments, Masako felt a deep, loving attachment for the finely woven materials. Although on the surface she was living in the busy modern world, she felt that in her heart she belonged to an older, more elegant age.

"People say that in ancient times they wore the old hunting costume in the Yabusame, I wonder when they changed over to the armor they wear now?" asked Shizuka as she brought out the hunting robe and laid it before Takeji.

"I'm not interested in learning about old costumes like that," replied Takeji as he received the robe.

"Takeji prefers the hunting robe even though everyone else wears armor; he specially requested to be allowed to wear the more courtly hunting robe," explained Shizuka to Masako.

The horse's elaborate trappings were arranged by Kō-ichi. It is said that the horse's gear is simpler now than it was in the olden days, but even so, it takes some practice to be able to mount the Chinese saddle and ride.

When Takeji had gotten the hunting robe on, he donned a pair of chaps made of deer skin. Then he put on leather stockings, a wrist guard on his left arm, and leather gloves. Finally, putting on his cap, he went into the entry hall. There he put on a helmet over his hat and tightened the chin strap. He put on boots. Finally he slung on his quiver loaded with five forked arrows and six bulbed arrows. He strapped on a long sword, tucked a dagger in his belt, and grasping the Shigetō bow, he mounted Phoenix. Masako had known Takeji ever since she had come to this house as a bride and she felt as though his figure now in this ancient and formal costume summed up all the thoughts and feelings she had had for him over the years. As she watched, she felt glowing perfectly within herself Takeji's words when he said that by learning archery he had discovered a Yabusame of his own. Ever since the day she had heard from Shizuka that her husband was returning, she had felt stirring within her something of the discipline that governed Takeji. During those five days her life as a woman had come to an end and she had seen a vision of her own death, and yet Masako felt that there was something in those five days that would never fade.

"Are you coming later?" asked Takeji from the horse.

"Yes, we'll be along soon," replied Shizuka. "There will be many people in the street today, so be careful with the horse."

Masako opened the gate.

"You'll be coming later, won't you?"

"No. I'll stay home today and look after the house."

"Why?"

"Just concentrate on shooting the targets, Takeji, don't think about anything else. The one wish I have in my heart is that you will never give up archery."

"What do you mean?"

"That's my one wish."

"Are you saying I should devote my full attention to archery and nothing else?"

"That's right. The world is filled with flying planes and

racing cars, but the one beautiful thing in the midst of all that activity is your motionless figure completely concentrating on the target the way you have learned through rigorous practice. That is probably the only enclave of beauty we can find in this modern age. I have been enthralled by that image of you ever since I became a part of this family. Good-bye."

The expression on Takeji's face said clearly that he did not understand, but at last he rode out the gate. The horse's footsteps echoed loudly in the sunlight along the drowzy, residential street and gradually faded in the distance.

A short while later Masako said good-bye to Kōichi, Shizuka, and the maid who were going to see the Yabusame. "Takehiko may return and it would be disconcerting to him if I am not here." This was the reason she gave for staying home that day.

After the others had left, Masako closed the gate and returned to the house where she sat looking out at the garden. The entire garden was bright with September sunlight and everywhere were clumps of late-blooming flowers announcing the arrival of autumn. The intimate fullness of those few days with Takeji remained in her heart with a richness that could never again be matched.

Masako drew from the bosom of her kimono a razor wrapped in tissue paper and placed it in front of her. Her heart was pained when she thought of the inconvenience this would cause the Kitōs who had done so much for her, and when she thought of the sadness it would cause her parents, but Masako was beyond the world of time and change and this was the only way for her to be herself. Her life meant nothing without the step she was about to take. By ending her own life she would simultaneously get revenge on her husband and prove her fidelity to Takeji.

With the razor in her right hand, Masako made a deep slash in her left wrist. A vast amount of blood spurted out and soaked into the tatami mats. Switching the razor to her left hand, she cut her right wrist. Laying the razor beside her, she gazed out at the sunlight in the garden.

Time seemed to pass quickly. Soon it appeared to grow dark and she began to feel dizzy. A few moments later she fell forward and everything grew dark. Then far away through the darkness Masako heard the sound of hoofbeats approaching. As the hoofbeats thundered nearer, there was another sound. There was the quick snap of an arrow being released, the long hum of the arrow cutting through the air, the short smack as it hit the target. Two short sounds and a long sound, this pure sound repeated again and again in the sunlight reverberated with infinite richness within Masako's heart.

A moment later everything went dark.

TORCHLIGHT NŌ

1

The Mibu family had two sons; both were now dead. The elder son had died during the war leaving behind a young widow and a daughter. Before long the attractive widow remarried and left the Mibu family. The daughter, Masako, was left behind to be raised by her paternal grandfather.

The second of the Mibu sons had already left home, but returned at the time of his brother's death to take over as head of the family. He survived the war only to die in the spring of 1946. One evening, at the black market on the south side of Kamakura station, he became involved in a quarrel over some trivial matter with an American soldier. The soldier shot him with a pistol, and he was dead at the age of thirty-four. He left behind a lovely young widow and a son. At the urging of her parents, however, the widow left the Mibu family the following year and remarried. She took her son with her to her new family, but the boy, Shuntarō, did not get along with his new father. One day in early summer he set out for school as usual, but never returned. After school he had gone to his grandfather's house in Kamakura and decided to live there.

Pleased, the grandfather, Tokinobu, declared that this was quite natural, and decided to adopt the boy and raise him along with Masako. His idea was to have Shuntarō succeed him one day as head of the Mibu family. The boy's mother made several trips between Tokyo and Kamakura and soon agreed to this arrangement.

Shuntarō was nine; Masako, thirteen that year. In the end they lived together as brother and sister for twelve years until the autumn of Masako's twenty-fifth year when she married Kōzō Izumi.

For three generations the Mibu family had owned a store in Nihonbashi that imported woolen goods. After 1941, they had not been able to import goods, and after the war there was little prospect of rebuilding their once prosperous business. No sooner had Tokinobu resigned himself to the thought that it would probably be a decade at least before free trade developed to the level it had been on before, than he lost his second son. At that point he quickly sold the store and retired to his home in Kamakura.

Shuntarō was the only hope that remained for the declining fortunes of the Mibu family. Two months after Masako was married in the winter of Shuntarō's twenty-first year, Tokinobu died, leaving many anxieties unresolved. All this happened in 1959. By then the old family home at Inamuragasaki in Kamakura had passed into other hands. All that remained for Shuntarō was a Nō pavilion standing on a small plot of land behind the main house. He continued living there for some four years.

2

In Kamakura in the early fall every year there is a performance of the Takiginō. This is a Nō performance at night on an outdoor stage lighted only by flaming torches. Toward the end of August, Masako learned that this year's Takiginō would be performed on September twenty-second. She learned this one day when she was out shopping; on her way home she had stopped at the Genjidō, a shop that specialized in Kamakura's famous wood carvings. It was a chilly day and the streets retained only faint traces of summer.

The Genjidō had a raised floor in the traditional Japanese style. Sitting on the edge of this raised area, Masako enjoyed a cup of excellent tea served to her by the shopkeeper's wife. It was then she noticed a poster on the wall announcing this year's Takiginō. Masako's visit to the shop was entirely casual; for the past four years she had been in the habit of dropping in here from time to time for a cup of tea and a chat. She had first come here on a bright sunny autumn day just four years ago, the year she married Kōzō Izumi, and she had continued the custom since then. As she sipped her tea, Masako looked again at the poster. The performance was to be held, as usual, at the Kamakura Shrine at Daitōnomiya.

Four years ago Masako had attended the Takiginō with her grandfather and her cousin. Two months later she had married Kōzō, and two months after that her grandfather had passed away. In the first two years of her marriage her husband had attended the performance with her, but he had very little interest in the Nō, and last year she had gone to the performance alone.

Seeing Nō performances was a cultivated taste that had always been a part of Masako's life. She remembered growing up at Inamuragasaki where her grandfather had once danced three consecutive performances on the Nō stage that was now all that remained of the family estate. Her grandfather had stayed vigorous by eating broiled eels every day of his life until just before he died at the age of seventy-nine. From childhood Masako had watched Nō performances and had studied the dance movements, and so had developed a good understanding and appreciation of the Nō. She remembered several of her grandfather's performances that were comparable in excellence to those of a professional Nō actor of the first rank.

On a shelf inside the Genjidō were three Nō masks Masako had seen there a month earlier. All three depicted the faces of noble women. One was the correct and dignified Zōonna whose features expressed the restrained formality of a married woman. Another, by contrast, was a beautiful Fushikizō that expressed youthfulness tempered by experience. The third was an elegant Magojirō with its gentle charm suggesting a combination of fragility with a hint of passion.* For the past four years, whenever Masako had confronted such masks, it had really been an encounter with her cousin Shuntarō Mibu who had carved them.

"Can these be the same masks I saw here in July?" Masako asked the shopkeeper's wife.

"Only the Fushikizō was here in July," replied the

woman looking up at the masks. "We sold the others. The two new ones arrived about ten days ago."

'In that case,' thought Masako, 'Shuntarō must still be trying to make a living by carving masks.'

"Mr. Mibu drops in once in a while," said the shopkeeper's wife. "Every time he comes he grumbles that the masks don't sell well. My husband tries to talk him into carving something else, but he just smiles and says, 'Well, maybe someday, but not right now.' "

After having another cup of tea, Masako left the Genjidō. The afternoon sunlight dappled the ground in the shade of the cherry trees. Walking along the elevated promenade toward the station, Masako recalled her childhood days when she and Shuntarō had played "show each other." In this game the children would take off their clothes and examine each other's bodies from the waist down. Sometimes Shuntarō would even touch or caress Masako, but she never touched him. Even as a child she felt it would be bad to "touch a boy."

They found deserted rooms in the large house or secluded corners in garden where they could play their game.

Shortly before she married Kōzō, Shuntarō had asked her, "Do you remember when we used to play 'show each other?' Children today probably don't do that any more, but I still remember the sensation I had when I touched you. You were so soft and plump and white as porcelain."

Walking toward the station Masako wondered to herself, 'Why do I keep remembering these incidents from my childhood? I wonder if memories always just pop into one's mind suddenly like this? Maybe it's just that as Shuntarō and I grow further apart, all that remains are the memories, so they become sharper and more clearly focused.' Again Masako's thoughts went back to her cousin; she especially remembered his eyes. Shuntarō Mibu did not resemble either of his parents and his features were almost ugly, but he had clear, forthright eyes. As a youth he was on the college soccer team, and when he returned home from school, he spent his time carving Nō masks. In everything he did, he preferred things that were clear and simple. Masako recalled that even in the chaotic days following the war, the nine year old boy had been intent on carving Nō masks. Even now as she walked along it occurred to Masako that such a boy was very unusual these days.

In the game of soccer Shuntarō had found the virtues of order, control, and courage. The strenuous physical exercise and the level of tension required to win were everything to him. Why would such a person continue to be interested in carving Nō masks? Masako had asked her cousin about this after she had become engaged to Kōzō Izumi. Masako believed that soccer and mask carving were conflicting interests. In her opinion, mask carving and soccer detracted from each other. He only smiled and said nothing. There was an ancient Nō mask hanging in his grandfather's Nō pavilion, and it may be that he found in this mask some likeness to his mother who had married into another family. Having willfully left his mother's side, he could not now abandon his grandfather's house.

Almost as soon as she had married Kōzō, Masako

began to wonder if she could ever live apart from her cousin. Although she had expected to miss Shuntarō to some extent, she had not expected that her life with Kōzō would be so completely empty. She had no particular reason to be dissatisfied with her husband, but at night, even as she gave herself to him, her thoughts would drift back to the Nō pavilion and to the homely boy who carved his Nō masks there.

At their grandfather's funeral she had caught hold of her cousin and made him promise that he would not marry until she had borne her first child. Time passed and Masako's emptiness increased. That was four years ago now and this emptiness threatened to engulf her like the need for love. After four years Masako still had not borne a child. Several times since the previous spring she had considered visiting her cousin. She had even gone partway once but had changed her mind. What stopped her was not her fear of being an unfaithful wife, but the realization that as cousins she and Shuntarō were related by blood.

This year again, Masako looked forward to September twenty-second with secret anticipation. And yet when the day arrived, she did not go see the Takiginō after all. Thinking about it later, she understood that she alone knew the real reason she had not gone. It was simply that since her marriage to Kōzō she had never seen her cousin at the performance. Their situation was not much different from that of the herd boy and the weaving maiden. According to the old legend, these two stars meet but once a year.

One Sunday afternoon in early October, Masako and

Kōzō were walking together on Rokujizō Avenue. As they passed a notice board, Kōzō saw a poster for the Takiginō and said, "You didn't go to the Takiginō this year, did you?"

"That's right," replied Masako gracefully. "I gave it up this year." But even as she said it, she felt a twinge of guilt.

And so the year drew uneventfully to a close, but in the heart of this young housewife the fires of the Takiginō still blazed, carving their pattern on the darkness of the night itself.

The year Masako and Kōzō were married, the Kamakura Takiginō was officially established as an annual public event; it had not been, previously. But Masako had seen Takiginō before. The first time had been on a trip to Nara with her grandfather and Shuntarō; they had seen the performance at the Kofukuji Temple. Masako was eighteen that year. Even before that, however, she had sensed in her cousin something of eternal value to her.

3

It was Masako's custom every year in mid-April to go to the Nō theatre in Meguro in Tokyo to see a performance of the play *Sotoba Komachi*. Her grandfather had always said, "To see the Nō and to perform the dances are suitable arts for a woman to cultivate. But if you choose to do these things, you ought never to be ostentatious about it, nor should a woman try to earn her living by doing it." He said this because he found female performers distasteful on the Nō stage. He said they distorted the rigorous order required for the dance. He said it was offensive to see them on the stage. Masako, however, was indifferent to all this. She considered it a luxury for a woman to cultivate the Nō and conducted herself accordingly. Consequently, even though she did study the dance movements, she never appeared in the seasonal performances for amateurs.

As it turned out, Masako met her cousin at the Nō theatre in Meguro at the performance of *Sotoba Komachi,* and later she was never really certain whether or not it had just been a coincidence that brought them together. She knew he went to the theatre in Meguro occasionally, but oddly enough they had never before been there on the same day.

"We haven't seen each other in a long time; why don't you treat me to dinner. I'm broke at the moment," said Shuntarō. Masako was delighted to see her cousin behaving like this.

They left the theatre at seven o'clock without seeing the final performance. Taking the Tōyoko Line to Yokohama, they decided to go to Chinatown to eat in a Chinese restaurant. Her husband had gone to Atami where he would be spending the night at a celebration honoring faculty members from his university.

It may seem strange to some that although Masako and Shuntarō had both lived in Kamakura all this time, they had never met in the four years since their grandfather's funeral. They had both been reticent in expressing their affection for each other, but neither of them had tried to avoid a meeting.

Shuntarō ate his food and drank his beer at an alarming speed, but still managed between mouthfuls to ask, "You still don't have any kids?"

"Have you found someone you want to marry yet?"

"No, it's not that, but—"

"That's certainly a vague answer—but no, I don't have any children."

"You aren't trying to avoid having children, are you?"

"I'm embarassed! How can you calmly sit there and ask someone something personal like that? You certainly have become bad mannered. If you really must know, Kōzō is sterile. He had mumps as a child and it caused him to become sterile. We only discovered this two years ago. The doctor explained everything to us. He said only one man in a thousand who gets mumps becomes sterile."

"That's interesting. I'm surprised it still happens in this age of advanced medicine."

"Are you feeling sorry for Kōzō or for me?"

"I'm impressed with those odds, a thousand to one. He's obviously one of the chosen few. It seems that many of the university professors I know are sterile. I wonder if all of them had mumps? It's really remarkable, isn't it—that there are so many university professors like that."

"Oh, come on! People don't get that way just because they are university professors—You know, you are just like you were in the old days; you haven't changed a bit."

"Did you suppose I'd changed?"

"I've wondered about it. I thought you'd become a recluse living all alone like that."

"I'm twenty-five. I'm too old to be feeling sorry for myself. You must be thirty-two or three by now."

"Don't be rude. I'm twenty-nine. Let's change the subject. What are you doing for a living these days?"

"I do whatever I can to get by. Once when I was really desperate, I nearly sold all of grandfather's Nō masks and robes. But then the Genjidō helped me out."

"The war has been over for eighteen years. It seems the Mibu family is the only one that has not gotten back on its feet."

"Don't let that bother you. Everything goes in cycles. By the way, you haven't seen me play soccer in a long time. Would you like to?"

"Isn't it about time you gave up soccer? I met Mr. Fukuda once and he mentioned that you were going to give it up."

"I did give it up once. After I graduated from college I thought I'd get a job and bring home a monthly salary and live an ordinary life just like everyone else. But look at me now. I've become disreputable. It all started last year when I was living like a hermit, as you call it, and I became very discouraged. I could not recall the face of our dear grandfather, or even the face of my beautiful mother I haven't seen since childhood. But I did remember very nostalgically the hot, sunlit soccer field. I wondered if I could ever regain the healthy vigor of my school days. So, I started playing soccer again."

"Did you ever try to think of me?"

"What would be the point of thinking of another man's wife?"

"Didn't you know how I felt about you?"

"To tell the truth, I walked past your house three different times. That was before all this happened I just told you about."

In her heart Masako was deeply touched, but outwardly she asked a very feminine question, "In that case, why didn't you come to the Takiginō if you wanted to see me? You promised you would. That was to be the one day of the year we would meet. Why did you waste it?"

"Two years ago was the only time I didn't go."

"You mean the time I went with Kōzō for the second year in a row?"

"I watched from a distance; all I saw was a woman who had become another man's wife."

"Since I'd never seen you there I decided not to go last year. I thought it would be too dreary. But two years ago I went by myself."

"That's life."

"Perhaps you're right."

Masako looked down at her plate. Apparently Shuntarō's feelings for her had not changed. A moment later she raised her eyes and asked where he would be playing soccer.

"At the Chichibunomiya Rugby Field on Sunday."

"I'll try to arrange to be there—You know, you really have become rather rude since I last knew you; I've felt it ever since we met this afternoon."

"You said that already. Maybe it's the way I dress."

"It's the way you look. You have a dissolute look in your eyes. All afternoon I've been thinking you must be seeing a bad woman."

"No," exclaimed Shuntarō just a little too quickly, "I've kept myself pure and innocent."

4

Three days a week Kōzō Izumi would leave home at seven in the morning. When his lectures were in the afternoon on the other three days, he left home at eleven. He walked down a slope, then followed the tracks of the Yokosuka Line north for three hundred meters until he reached Kita Kamakura Station. He would take the train to Tokyo Station then transfer to a local line as far as Ochanomizu. The trip from his home to the university took one hour and forty-five minutes. This had been his daily routine for ten years.

"Will you be home tomorrow afternoon? I have to go out for dancing practice." It was Saturday morning and Masako was talking to her husband as she saw him off at the front gate.

"I have a seminar scheduled for tonight. If it runs late, I'll stay over at Tsukiji, but I'll be back by tomorrow afternoon." Kōzō spoke in a remarkably pleasant voice; he was usually grouchy in the morning.

He had taught English literature at a private university in Kanda for a decade and if he put in a few more years,

he expected to be promoted to full professor. He was
well thought of as an intellectual, but that was of little
concern to Masako. Kōzō Izumi's one regret was that he
had not obtained a position in a prestigious national university; still, he had the respect of his friends and colleagues. Masako, however, merely saw him as a man
who embodied the widespread stereotype of a university professor with progressive ideas. There was a group
of faculty wives that met regularly, but Masako never attended their meetings. It was not that she found their
meetings boring, she simply was not interested in that
sort of activity.

Kōzō had what he called his "office" in Tsukiji. Masako
understood what motivated him to maintain this so-
called office; he had been born and raised in that down-
town section of Tokyo and still had deep feelings for it.
His family had operated a seafood store in Tsukiji. After
his father died, Kōzō had moved to the family's summer
home along with his mother and sister. They had left the
store to be run by the head clerk. During the war, however, the store had been destroyed in the fire bombing
and all the clerks killed, even the dog and cat they kept
as pets. After the war his mother decided to stay on in
Kamakura, and since Kōzō himself had no interest in re-
establishing the store, he sold the land, and the family
stayed in their summer house in Kamakura. Except for
the fact that there were snakes around, Kōzō was quite
content living in Kamakura.

As a scholar, Kōzō had written three books, and as a
person, he was a mild man in his mid-forties. In short,
he was a man with no outstanding faults. His mother

had died seven years earlier and his sister was married.

"Recently you've been staying over in Tsukiji quite a lot."

"I've been busy. Will your dancing practice be in Kamakura tomorrow?"

"No, it's in Tokyo."

She could not just casually tell her husband she was really going to watch her cousin play soccer. Some time ago he had expressed some suspicions about the kind of relationship she had had with her cousin before she was married. He believed that since they had lived together from childhood for more than ten years, some sort of affectionate relationship was bound to have developed. After all, he pointed out, they were cousins. Instead of defending her cousin in the face of her husband's accusations, Masako remained silent because she felt sorry for Shuntarō who had to live alone. Another reason she remained silent was that she felt she really loved her husband even though theirs had been an arranged marriage. But when his wife failed to make a satisfactory response to his charges, Kōzō felt that his suspicions were confirmed.

Having seen her husband off, Masako began to think how long it seemed until she would see her cousin at the soccer game the next day. Suddenly she decided to visit him at Inamuragasaki. Three times he had come right to the door of her house only to turn away for fear of making things awkward for her. She felt terribly rude for having neglected Shuntarō and wanted to make up for it.

Masako changed clothes, touched up her makeup, and left the house. On the train she decided it would be nice

to take him something to eat. She got off at Kamakura
and went to a *sushi** shop, but it was still too early and
the shop was closed. She ended up going to a coffee shop
where she bought sandwiches to take out. Returning to
the station she got a ticket for Inamuragasaki and went
through the underground passage to the platform for the
Enoshima Line. As she waited for the train she changed
her mind about visiting her cousin. This was not a sudden decision; the thought had been in the back of her
mind ever since she had been in the coffee shop getting
the sandwiches. She had been thinking about those misgivings her husband had expressed several years earlier.
At that time, as a result of his suspicions, he had become
jealous and had completely devoted himself to Masako
who was thirteen years his junior. But what brought Masako to a halt more than anything else was her realization that there was more than mere sympathy in her
feelings for Shuntarō. Masako was aware of the conflict
between their close relationship as cousins and the feelings of love and affection they had for each other. Over
the years this conflict had intensified. For some time she
had been conscious of the dissolute look in her cousin's
eyes. Masako realized that to go see Shuntarō tomorrow
at a soccer game was very different from going to him
like this today. Besides, Masako felt she still loved her
husband. 'After not visiting Shuntarō for all these years,
what would be gained by being unfaithful to my husband now?' she wondered as she left the station.

Having time on her hands and nothing else to do, Masako stopped at the Genjidō.

"Why, Mrs. Izumi, are you out shopping so early?" exclaimed the owner's wife from the raised part of the shop as Masako entered. The woman seemed to be smiling in a knowing way and Masako felt as though her secret feelings had been discovered. She began to blush, and in order to hide her embarassment, she asked to see some saucers.

As the shopkeeper's wife was arranging several kinds of saucers for her to examine, Masako looked up at the shelf where the Nō masks were displayed. There were five of them now; a Deigan and a Koomote* had been added. Masako had no way of knowing when the two new masks had gone on display, but it was clear to her that her cousin was continuing to do the work he liked best. In the presence of these masks, a new feeling stirred within her heart, 'Maybe I'm being too defensive about my husband to Shuntarō.' With this thought Masako felt that she was miserable and alone.

She ended up buying five saucers she did not want, but after leaving the Genjidō she felt exhilarated by having seen Shuntarō's masks. She looked forward eagerly to seeing him on the soccer field the next day.

The spring afternoon dragged on and on. For some weeks now Masako had noticed how long the afternoons had become. On those days when her husband did not return home, she was even more keenly aware of how long the days could be. She felt such days with her whole being, and when her husband stayed over in Tsukiji on such a day, the night seemed interminable; she physically felt the strain. At sunset she could hear the temple bells from the nearby Enkakuji and the Tokeiji which faced each other across the narrow valley. These

bells struck a disturbing feeling within her heart, especially on afternoons when she knew her husband would
not be returning home. It made her wonder why she
went on living. It seemed to her this feeling was somehow connected with the decline of the Mibu family and
its fortunes.

There was a fixed order for the tolling of the sonorous
bells. First the great bell at the Enkakuji would toll a
tone so deep and rich that it seemed to hang in the air
like a physical presence. Before one quite realized that
the sound had gone, the bell at the Tokeiji would re-
spond. Again today she could hear the tolling of the bell
at the Enkakuji and with it came the thought that her
husband would not be returning that night. She was
sorry now that she had not gone to visit her cousin after
all. She felt that it was not really such a serious matter.
She nibbled at the sandwiches she had planned to take
to Shuntarō, but they were tasteless. She wondered how
many evenings she had spent like this. It was at such
moments that she seriously began to wonder whether or
not she really loved her husband. Occasionally he would
return home unexpectedly after he had said he would be
away all night. But even then happiness did not always
flood her heart at the moment of his return. Sometimes
it seemed to her that she did not love her husband as
much as she thought she did. Masako herself felt that
such moments were dangerous.

Often after a long and boring day, Masako only
wanted to get in bed beside her husband and sleep a
deep, dreamless sleep. It seemed her thoughts dwelled
on this more and more since her marriage. She kept re-

turning to the thought that once their sexual desire had spent itself, they returned to a hollow pretense of love so faint that they themselves were hardly aware of it. All this was not mere introspection; it suggested some imbalance within her. This was not the insecurity of the ordinary housewife; it came from her being the daughter of a venerable old family whose fortunes had declined. She had often felt that there was no longer a place for her in this world. At such moments her mind would fill with an image of the flaming torches of the Takiginō carving their patterns on the darkness of the night.

5

Apparently there had been a change in Kōzō's plans, for he returned late that night. Masako felt flustered and upset by this, as though she had been discovered at a secret rendezvous with a lover. Even though she had endured the tedium of a long afternoon, there had been no sense of anticipation for her husband's return. That evening she had gone to bed early, looking forward to the following day. She had let her mind drift to thoughts of the playing field on a spring day and the image of an athletic young man moving swiftly across it.

Overcoming her initial consternation, Masako merely felt annoyed at her husband's early return. She prepared his bedding while he bathed, and as she worked it occurred to her that she had never before experienced these feelings of guilty panic and annoyance when her husband returned home. This thought surprised her. 'As Shuntarō pointed out,' she thought, 'I am a married woman. Why should I be so upset by this?'

The next day Masako went to the soccer game as she had planned. Kōzō told her he was expecting guests that evening and asked her to be home by four o'clock. She made what preparations she could in the morning before she left. She was forty minutes late by the time she got to the playing field, and the game had already started. There were perhaps a hundred spectators in the stands; Masako sat on a bench at some distance from them.

She easily picked out Shuntarō from among the agile players on the field. He broke away from the group and ran, dribbling the ball with his right and left feet. Two other players suddenly descended on him for a tackle, but at the last moment Shuntarō kicked the ball with the inside of his right foot. His long leg stretched out at a sharp angle and for a moment it seemed as though he would score, but then another youth intercepted the ball with his foot. Masako was aroused by the virile movements of these youths as they moved back and forth in the bright spring sunlight. Watching their movements, Masako shared the feeling Shuntarō had expressed earlier, the feeling of having regained in her life something that had been lost. The image of Shuntarō that Masako kept in her heart had not wavered over the years and even now it remained unchanged.

With her eyes Masako followed the movements of the players, but her mind drifted in daydreams; occasionally a loud shout from the playing field disturbed her serenity and called her attention back to the game. At the university Shuntarō had played the position of left inner, but Masako had no idea what position he was playing now. According to the scoreboard the competitors were members of the alumni association. From time to time a gust of wind caused a swirl of dust to dance across the field. Masako did not pay much attention to the game, but merely watched the patterns of movement and let her mind wander.

The next thing she knew, the game was over and her cousin was walking toward her from the bright, sunlit field. He was covered with dirt and his eyes shone in his sweat-drenched face. Masako was aware of his sweaty, animal smell when he sat down beside her. She felt rising within her some of the happiness she had known when they had been living together.

"It's been a long time since I've seen you like this." At this moment Masako had forgotten all about her husband. She felt as though she had escaped from the real world and had returned to her earlier self.

"I feel very happy right now," said Shuntarō wiping the sweat from his face with his arm. It had been a long time since Masako had seen such clear, forthright eyes.

"Now that the game is over, I expect you will be going out somewhere with the rest of the players."

"No. I'm going to skip that. I want you to treat me to a good meal. It's been a long time since I had some of your cooking, but I guess I'll have to do without that today. Anyway, I'd better go shower," said Shuntarō getting to his feet.

"I'm sorry, Shuntarō, but I have to go home now. Kōzō

is expecting guests this evening." Masako was sure she would never make it back on time if she took her cousin out to dinner first.

"I see," said Shuntarō coldly. He was clearly disappointed.

"I'll make it up to you. I promise I'll come visit you very soon."

"What do you mean by that? I don't mind if you come, but—"

"Well, I've never been back for a visit, not once since grandfather's funeral and—and yesterday I saw some of your masks at the Genjidō."

"Well, thanks. When shall I expect you?"

"I can't promise an exact date right now."

"You can't promise an exact date—I see. Well, I won't get my hopes up then. I'll just go on carving masks when I feel in the mood for it and throw myself into a game of soccer once in a while. That's enough for me. That's all the sympathy I need."

"Stop talking like that!"

"Do you think I'm just sulking? If you do, you'd better go clean your ears. And if you think I'm being sarcastic, it just proves your mind isn't as pure as you like to think. The other day you said I had a dissolute look in my eyes, but really, I haven't changed a bit. I may be a little vulgar, I'll admit that." With that Shuntarō simply waved goodbye and walked away.

Masako watched her cousin's broad back as he strode across the playing field, but he disappeared into the locker room without looking back. Masako intended to wave if he looked back, but when she thought about it, there was no reason for him to turn back. After all, he had left his mother at the age of nine and he hadn't looked back then. She realized now that he had been more disappointed than she had expected and her heart ached. She wanted to call him back and take him out to dinner, but of course that was not possible. This was partly because she had thought about her own situation of the past few days, and she had become alarmed by the feelings she had for her cousin. So far there was nothing wrong with their relationship, but there was no mistaking what could happen if she spent much time with him feeling the way she did.

When she looked around, all the other spectators had gone. Masako, too, stood up and left.

As she left the playing field and walked toward the subway station, her mind pursued a vague, but beautiful dream. Certainly her meeting with Shuntarō had affected her, a feeling she could not shake off. For some reason, at the same time she also remembered her husband's loving caresses from the previous night. On the one hand her body still tingled from her husband's touch, and on the other hand, she could see in her mind the clear, forthright eyes of the young man. Masako suddenly felt very self-conscious and looked around to see if anyone was watching. She felt like a wanton woman.

She took the subway to Shibuya and went to the Tōyoko Department Store. In the grocery department she ordered a bottle of whiskey and an assortment of canned meats and asked that they be delivered to her cousin's address. She did this to make up for not taking him to dinner.

Masako got home just at four o'clock, but Kōzō and his guests were already there drinking beer. The visitors were colleagues who also taught English at the same university. For some reason these four spoke English whenever they got together. Masako found this a bit curious. When she saw the four together, Masako would make a mental comparison between them and her grandfather and cousin. She kept an aloof smile as she watched her husband, but in her heart she felt something almost like remorse that no one in the Mibu family had been quite so ambitious. It was not just that these university professors discussed only the most commonplace things, but rather it was her pride in being a member of the Mibu family that made her feel out of place and uncomfortable with these men. Yet in a sense these men were the elite, the ones who would surely succeed most brilliantly in the modern world. In fact, Masako was impressed with the speed at which these men could change their beliefs and attitudes to stay in step with current trends.

6

At last it was summer. Masako still had not gone to visit her cousin at Inamuragasaki. Since spring she had devoted all her attention to her husband; in this respect she was determined to be a model wife.

Twice she had visited the Genjidō to see the Nō masks; once in late May and once again in early July. For five years she had been going to see the masks, finding some small satisfaction in doing this. By now it had almost become a habit, and she went without feeling self-conscious. Her cousin found happiness in carving Nō masks and by throwing himself into his soccer games, and to the same degree Masako enjoyed her own satisfactions. No matter how she looked at it, she felt out of place in the modern world. 'Look at Kōzō and his friends, and even his friends' wives – they all know how to enjoy life. If a prominent foreign musician came to town, they would all go to the concert; if a well-reviewed movie was showing, they would go there. There were parties, trips, skiing – they all enjoy the giddy whirl of social life.' Masako, on the other hand, quietly cultivated herself by attending performances of the Nō dance, and by going from time to time to see the Nō masks at the Genjidō. In many ways her daily life was quite divorced from the real world. Still, her relationship with Kōzō was improving. During that spring and early summer there were even moments in bed at night when she was consumed by the burning pleasure she felt in her husband's arms. She wondered if it was her growing maturity that increased these new sensations.

Shortly after the university recessed in mid-July for the summer holiday, Kōzō was invited to give a lecture series at the summer session of a school in Shinshū. He planned to be away for ten days.

After her husband had gone, there was a succession of

unusually hot days. Masako's room was unbearably hot. In the midst of this heat she longed for the dizzying pleasure she had found with her husband. She did not know what to do with herself. At this point she could see clearly how things stood between her and her husband. Her inner uncertainty had been transformed into sexual desire and for the time being that had been satisfied. But now that her sexual partner was no longer there with her, a peculiar loneliness came over her heart. She was sad that she would not see her husband for ten days. The fact that he was not with her made her think back fondly on their five years together. Still, she had to face the fact that she did not love this man who had aroused in her an intense awareness of physical pleasure. There was bitterness in this realization.

On the morning of the eleventh day, Masako got up at eight o'clock as usual. The morning sunlight glittered through the leaves of the trees surrounding the house and spots of sunlight dappled the ground. The cicadas had already begun their chorus announcing the advent of another long day. As she gazed at this scene, an unaccountable sense of lassitude came over her. Masako felt the ripe fullness of her body and wondered why her husband had left her alone and unfulfilled for ten days. Several days before, she had received a post card from him, but he had not returned on the evening of the tenth day as he had planned.

Masako looked into her husband's study. On the desk lay a copy of his most recent book just published this summer. The book had the extraordinarily long title, *The Influence of America's New Criticism in England.* Seeing this long title only heightened Masako's malaise. At this point she made up her mind to leave the hot, stuffy countryside and to go have a look at the kind of "office" Kōzō kept in Tokyo.

She had seen her husband in his surroundings at home and thought it would be amusing to see what sort of place he kept in Tokyo. The fact is she was bored and thought this would be a way to help pass the time. There was nothing else to do and she needed something to occupy her mind. During the ten days she had been alone, she had three times considered going to see her cousin. Each time she talked herself out of it.

Masako ate a simple breakfast and changed into a brand new linen kimono with a hand woven brocade *obi.* Shortly after nine she took up her parasol and left the house.

She had been to her husband's study once before when he had first rented it. It was located in a small Japanese-style inn adjoining a small restaurant in Tsukiji on a narrow street between Saint Luke's Hospital and the Kyō-bashi Metropolitan High School. From Tokyo Station she took a bus that let her off quite near the place. The street was sweltering in the summer sun as she walked from the bus stop to the restaurant. Entering from the gate, she met the landlady who was seeing off one of the overnight guests.

"Well, look who's here! Please come in, Mrs. Izumi. I understand your husband is in Shinshū."

Masako froze when she heard this greeting. She knew intuitively that the landlady was concealing something. It occurred to Masako that if Kōzō had told the landlady he was going to Shinshū for ten days, she should have asked whether he had returned yet or not.

"He sent a note from Shinshū asking me to send him a book he left here. I came to pick it up." This was the best reply Masako could come up with. She could not help thinking her husband might have stayed here the night before and suddenly her mind was filled with all the doubts and suspicions she had had about him in the past.

"Please come in. You must be very hot after coming all the way from Kamakura. We were very crowded last night so I went ahead on my own and let another guest sleep in Professor Izumi's room. I didn't think he would mind. It's being cleaned right now; it will be just a moment till they get everything in order. Please wait here."

Feeling the woman's explanation was too elaborate to be true, Masako slipped off her sandals and entered the inn. While the landlady was away asking the maid to bring Masako a cup of tea, Masako started up the stairs to the second floor. As she reached the top of the stairs, the woman below cried out in alarm, "Mrs. Izumi! Wait, please." There was something unnatural about the way she said it, and this triggered Masako's next move. She slid open the door to her husband's room. If they were really only cleaning it, it would not matter if she went in or not.

The first room was a small anteroom; her husband's summer suit was hanging against the wall. Draped over the clothes rack nearby were a woman's silk kimono and *obi*. Masako stood still with astonishment, her eyes fixed on the silk kimono. The landlady came up behind Masako and cupping a hand to her mouth whispered to Masako not to go any further. Seeing the alarm in the woman's eyes, Masako opened the door to the adjoining room. There was an open window screened by a green reed blind. Summer bedding had been laid out and there lying on their stomachs, side by side smoking, were a man and a woman. The woman looked up first; she was plump and had heavy eyebrows. She gave a cry of alarm causing Kōzō to turn around. Up to this point Masako's only feeling had been one of astonishment, but when she saw the miserable look on her husband's face, she was enraged. She marched straight into the room and stripped back the bedding. Pushing aside the reed blind, she threw the blanket out the window. Both the man and the woman were stark naked. The large woman jumped up and hurried out of the room crouching down to cover herself. Kōzō frantically clutched the sheet about his waist and shouted, "No! Wait!" Masako snatched up the underwear that was lying there and rolled it into a ball. Next she took her husband's suit and the woman's kimono and adding them to the ball went downstairs.

"Masako! Wait, you don't understand. You're making a mistake." His voice reached her, but she paid no attention. She could only think what a miserable, pathetic figure he made.

As Masako passed through the lobby she saw the woman, wearing a bathrobe now, whispering to the landlady. Seeing Masako, the other woman hurried away, but the landlady approached saying, "Please wait a moment, Mrs. Izumi. It was wrong of me to try to lie to you. Please wait a moment, we can straighten this out."

Without slowing down, Masako slipped on her sandals, took her parasol, and went out. She flung the bundle of clothes in a sewage ditch as she walked to the main street. Hailing a taxi she snapped at the driver to take her to Kamakura. She could not forgive her husband for the pathetic figure he made. Her pride had been wounded. All the way back to Kamakura she thought about her grandfather.

That evening Kōzō returned home accompanied by the landlady of the hotel. She presented a box of cakes and began to apologize.

"You don't have to apologize to me. You were just doing your job." Masako refused the cakes and sent the woman away. Her husband was wearing a new white shirt and a pair of trousers, apparently purchased that afternoon, that were far too large for him.

"You shouldn't feel jealous of that woman."

"What are you talking about? What makes you think I'm jealous of her? I don't even remember what she looks like."

"I returned from Shinshū last night. I know I should have come home first, but I just stopped there to pick up a book and I guess I had a little too much to drink."

"Stop it! I don't want to hear any of your excuses."

"It's the truth. I'm not trying to make excuses, it's just that—"

Kōzō continued trying to make excuses, but Masako remained silent. She paid no attention to what he said about the woman, or how it had all come about. Oddly enough, she did not feel the surge of jealousy she had expected. She merely wondered if everything that had happened in the last five years had really been as meaningless as it seemed now. Memories of the pleasure she had enjoyed with her husband since last spring quickly faded. 'So that was going on all the time.' She was suddenly overcome with remorse.

When his wife barged in on them at the hotel, Kōzō had shouted, "You don't understand," but in fact it was he who did not understand his wife. He had returned home feeling certain she would be jealous, and in so doing he had revealed another aspect of his character. Since his wife remained silent no matter what he said to her, he decided in desperation to force her to make love. She merely responded with a sneer in English, "Stop it, you pretentious bastard!" The statement surprised even Masako, for this was the kind of language she was determined never to use under any circumstances. Kōzō understood this and felt that at last he had broken through her wall of silence. "Sure," he grinned and took his bedding into the study to sleep.

Masako was still wondering what to make of his grin when he reappeared and said, "There are all kinds of women in this world, but you are really a strange one. I just can't figure you out." With that he returned to his study.

Masako did not sleep at all that night. At dawn she heard the song of a warbler and quite naturally thoughts of her grandfather came to mind. She remembered that he had once said to her, "A child raised in an antique shop is always surrounded by genuine antiques and he learns to spot a phoney right away. Kōzō is probably the real thing, but if you ever have a falling out with him, the best thing would be to just leave him." She wondered now if her grandfather had felt some misgivings about her marriage to Kōzō.

From that time on relations between Masako and her husband rapidly cooled. This was during the hottest part of the summer.

7

Kōzō Izumi began to stay out quite openly. He sometimes wore summer neckties that had been given to him by other women and changed his clothes, even his underwear, "over there." Masako always referred to it as "over there" though she had no idea where "over there" was. Masako knew her husband was, in fact, quite an attractive man even without his title of university professor, and she was not surprised that women found him appealing. At the same time, it was also clear that he was trying to patch things up with Masako, that he wanted to rebuild their marriage and regain his wife's attention. But Masako, on the other hand, had no interest in what these other women might think of her as a wife. She used the western-style living room as her bedroom and kept the door locked while she was asleep. Alone at night she had visions of the torchlight at the performance of the Takiginō. She could see her grandfather walking away from her and entering the Ikaruga Temple in silence. She did not know how changed her relationship with her husband was, but her thoughts were certainly more on her grandfather and Shuntarō and Shuntarō's father.

Early one morning Masako awakened to sensations she had nearly forgotten. Somehow Kōzō had gotten into the room and was lying beside her. Suddenly he was on top of her, and though she tried to resist she finally gave herself up to a flood of sexual passion. Afterwards, Masako lay in silence feeling the warm thrill of Kōzō's hand on her stomach. He admitted that for a time he had carried on a secret affair, but that now he wanted to come back to his wife. "When we were married," he said, "your parents were no longer around and some of my relatives were opposed to the match, but we've gotten along pretty well." He was being very practical. But feeling the cool morning breeze on her naked skin, Masako was overcome with an inexpressible sense of sadness and loneliness.

Now that this had happened, she felt she would no longer be able to reject her husband. She also knew they could not go on much longer together with nothing more than sex to sustain their relationship. When they could no longer save their marriage in bed, everything would be over anyway. Masako dozed again as her husband stroked and caressed her body. She made up her mind to visit Shuntarō. Now for the first time she had the courage to admit to herself her true feelings. The knowledge that her husband had been seeing another woman only made it easier for her.

Kōzō left the house shortly before ten o'clock saying he would be back that evening. For several weeks now

Masako had not bothered to ask where he was going when he went out. She had never imagined when they were married that things would ever reach this unhappy state. She was not interested in knowing where her husband was off to, but it seemed possible that today he was going to break off with the other woman. 'There is no point in doing that now,' thought Masako as she saw him off at the door.

She did some laundry, took a bath, and left the house. It was just noon.

8

This was the first time Masako had been back to Inamuragasaki since her grandfather's funeral. He had been buried at the Jufukuji Temple in Ōgigayatsu. He had been laid to rest there along with Masako's father who had died in the war and Shuntarō's father who had been killed by an American soldier. Every year she went to visit the graves. She always went alone, and she always felt sad and lonely. Her mother had remarried and was living in Odawara now, and Masako had only seen her once when she came to the wedding. She had heard that her mother had two children by her new husband. By now these children would be about the age Masako was when her mother abandoned her to her grandfather. On several occasions people had told her snatches of information about Shuntarō's mother. She was living in Tokyo with her new husband and three children. Perhaps out of deference to their new husbands, neither remarried woman had visited the graves. It was possible, of course, that they had made secret visits, but neither Masako nor Shuntarō had seen their mothers there.

Masako got off the train at Inamuragasaki and walked south until she came to the path leading up the mountain to her grandfather's house. She felt her chest tighten with emotion as she looked at the old familiar landscape in the glare of summer sunlight. One house even had the same bamboo fence exactly as it had been five years previously. The sun was directly overhead. As she climbed the mountain path, her progress was accompanied by a mounting sadness. It was here the family had seen her father off when he went to the war and here again a short time later his ashes had been sent to be interred at the temple. It was here she had said goodbye to her mother when she remarried. She had met Shuntarō here for the first time when his family moved in after their home was bombed, and a short time later they had said goodbye to Shuntarō's father, and then his mother, too, had left. After that she herself had gone away, down this same path with Kōzō, and almost immediately afterwards they had said farewell to her grandfather when his ashes were taken away to be buried. She felt as though the years and months, the changing seasons that had witnessed these events, were steeped with sadness.

Having reached the top of the slope, her body soaked with perspiration, she found herself standing before the old family home. Only a corner of the original house remained. The rest had been replaced by a modern two-story, reinforced concrete building enclosed by a white cement fence. On the second floor balcony was a noisy group of young people in bright-colored swimming suits. Jazz was blaring out from the house.

To get to the Nō pavilion Masako had to go around the new building to the back. She smelled fish cooking and there in the garden, in the shade of a large, old tree, she saw her cousin fanning a charcoal fire.

"So, you came after all." Shuntarō stood up and took a couple of steps toward her.

"Of course I came. I said I'd come, and I came."

"Let's eat. I just got back from catching these fish. The other day I caught a couple of greenlings over a foot long. I wish grandfather had been here to see that."

"I do too. I remember grandfather used to cook fish every day. Do you go fishing every day now?"

"Just about. All I have to buy are rice and vegetables and I can get by all right."

Both laundry and seaweed were drying on ropes strung between the trees in the garden.

"When was the old house torn down?"

"A year ago last spring. Recently they've been carrying on like this every day. I haven't been able to get anything done with all that noise."

"A concrete house and a concrete fence; it's really awful looking."

"That's the way things are these days. Do you remember the two girls who live there?"

"Yes, they must have graduated from college by now."

"The older one graduated two years ago. They've both become very good looking. They even come to visit me once in a while. The other day I almost got the older one in bed."

Masako reddened.

"Let's eat. The fish are done."

"I'm surprised at you. You really have gotten vulgar."

"Look Masako, it's nothing to worry about."

There was a long, narrow, Japanese-style room behind the Nō stage. In the past it had been used as a dressing room. Now Shuntarō slept there. What had once been the greenroom had a wooden floor and Shuntarō used it for his work room. Several masks he was making were lined up and there were also some trays he was carving.

"Are you making these trays to sell at Genjidō?"

"I started carving them because I needed the money, but it's boring work. I'm doing more detail work now, carving sash clips and brooches. I wonder if I would have become an ordinary office worker if grandfather had still been alive when I graduated from school?"

"It's sad to think of the past."

"Do you remember the time the three of us were walking in Nara?"

"How could I forget?"

"Then you remember what grandfather told us that day. 'A long time ago when your fathers were still in school, I came here with them and we walked down this very same street. Now both your fathers are dead and I am walking with my two grandchildren. I'm the only one still living.' I think I've come to understand the depth of sorrow grandfather must have felt as he told us that."

"Nothing has ever worked out for us, has it."

"I'm not complaining, but when you say something like that, I get the idea that things aren't going well for you and Kōzō. Are you trying to tell me your marriage isn't working out?"

"Yes."

"That's too bad, but I don't know anything about married life."

"We both live quite close to our mothers, but we can't even go to them for sympathy and support."

"Don't talk like that. I don't have any ill feelings toward my mother for going away and leaving me. I told myself I would not have any ill feeling toward her, and I like to think I've accomplished that. Do you remember that soccer game last spring? Well, not long after that I met my mother in Shinjuku."

Masako put down her chopsticks and stared at Shuntarō.

"It was quite unexpected, meeting her like that. I was on the second floor of the Nakamuraya restaurant. I was sitting next to the window waiting to meet a friend when I felt someone staring at me. I looked around and there she was off to my right about ten meters away. You can imagine the scene—a happy family excursion with the parents surrounded by their three children. I quickly turned away when I realized that this woman with her husband and children was my mother. I looked again to make sure. She quickly turned away and began talking to the children. When she looked up again a moment later, our eyes met. This time we both looked away. I considered the situation for a moment and decided to leave. I couldn't bring myself to go speak to her while

her husband and children were there. Besides, I didn't
think she would feel comfortable talking to her 'former'
son in the presence of her new family. So I moved to the
third floor. After I'd moved, though, I was afraid she'd
think I'd left because I still felt some resentment toward
her. I didn't want her to think that, so I wrote a note on a
paper napkin. It said, 'I didn't expect to see you here. I
want you to know that I didn't leave because I was
angry. Please understand.' I folded this up and gave it to
a waitress, asking her to give it to my mother when she
went to the lavatory by herself. The waitress agreed
without batting an eye. She came back later and told me
she had delivered the message without the rest of the
family knowing about it. The waitress probably just as-
sumed I was a young lover or something. In my mother's
other family, the oldest child is a daughter who must be
about fifteen, next is a boy about twelve, and the young-
est is a girl about eight. When I saw those children, I
realized that we all had the same mother, but somehow
it was more than just a gap of sixteen years that separated me from them. I didn't feel there was any chance of
bridging that gap. It is not as though we live far apart
and just happened to meet by accident; we actually live
very close to each other, but we have never met in sixteen years. That's why I reacted as I did."

"You've really grown up, haven't you. I'd never have
been able to think that fast."

"But after I got back home that day, I broke down and
cried. It went on and on. I couldn't seem to stop the
tears. I didn't want to see myself crying like that, so I
took grandfather's Nō mask off the wall and covered my

face with it. I looked in the mirror while I was wearing it. It was the Fushikizō. Since then I haven't felt like carving Nō masks anymore."

"Why not?"

"I don't know. I guess it was just bad luck accidentally to see my mother in the flesh like that. I had always supposed I would spend the rest of my life carving masks, but I know now that I won't. I don't know what to do now, I just feel empty inside."

"Doesn't playing soccer help you pull yourself together?"

"It used to – Shall I tell you another story?"

"What about? Is it something I should hear?"

"I don't know about that, but I'll tell you anyway. I'm twenty-five years old, and I've gotten into the habit of going every night to the market where my father was killed. I've been seeing a woman there. Do you want to hear about it?"

"If it's that kind of story, I don't want to hear it."

"I'll tell you anyway. Last spring when we met at the Nō theatre in Meguro, you asked if I'd been seeing bad women; well, by then I had already been seeing this woman for half a year. She's a widow, thirty-six years old. She's not especially good looking, but she has big breasts and big hips. She taught me all kinds of things."

"That's enough! I don't want to hear about it."

"When I'm with her, it's just like when I'm playing soccer. I don't have to think about anything. It is my last resort or refuge when I am feeling confused and don't know what to do."

"Do you love her?"

"I love her big tits and nice ass, and — "

"Stop it!" Masako stood up. She was afraid of what her cousin might say next.

"Hey, sit down. Listen to the rest of the story."

"It makes me sad to see you this way. You always used to be so strong and self-reliant."

"I'm not complaining and I'm not going to feel sorry for myself. The only sad thing is the fact that I've stopped carving masks. We saw the play *Sotoba Komachi* at Meguro. Do you remember the mask they used for the old woman's face? No matter how old she becomes there are no wrinkles and some of her youthful charm still remains. When I saw my mother that day, I was reminded of that mask and what a contrast it made to my mother's features. Meeting her unexpectedly like that after sixteen years, I had a very strong impression of her as dynamic and sexy. The pure, abstract image of her I had so carefully constructed was destroyed. But I suppose that if she were still my mother, I would feel proud that she had retained her youthful beauty that way."

"That would be selfish of you. Please tell me more about what your mother was like when you met her. I don't get a very clear picture of her when you only say she was 'dynamic and sexy.' "

"Well, as I just told you, she looked younger than she really is. Why should she feel obliged to make herself look so young? I was shocked to see her wearing a red suit; she must be in her late forties by now. I got the impression that she is a very energetic woman who likes lots of activity and who does everything in a big way. It was awful. Phoney. It might have been better if her red suit did not fit, or if it was old fashioned, but it looked like it fit perfectly."

"You told me you don't have anything to complain about, but you're complaining now. You used to be more tolerant of other people. It's not like you to be this way."

"I'm not really complaining. I'm just saying I don't like the Sotoba Komachi mask anymore."

"I think I'd better go home now."

"Don't you want to hear about my girlfriend?"

"No." Masako stood up again.

"Just because I've been seeing her doesn't mean I like her."

"I don't care. I don't want to hear about it. Tell me, Shuntarō, have you completely given up soccer?"

"Yes. The woman at the market does everything for me that soccer used to."

Masako left without replying to this.

"Masako, don't come back here again." At these words Masako paused for a moment, then went on without looking back.

Masako walked down the mountain path oblivious to the beauty of the sea spread out below. She could not bear the thought of her cousin fooling around with an older woman. The thought of him touching any woman other than herself was unbearable. She felt it would have been painful to know anything more about the woman. She tried to persuade herslef it was not exactly jealousy she felt, and yet the thought of Kōzō touching her body was also painful.

She got off the train at Kita Kamakura and walked home in the glaring sunlight. She thought of the expression on her cousin's face when he told her the woman was not particularly good looking, but that she had big breasts and hips. Masako felt trapped. On the one hand she could envision Kōzō's woman at the hotel in Tsukiji, and on the other hand she could imagine her cousin sleeping with the woman from the market. Her own position was intolerable.

9

Having the courage to go to Inamuragasaki was Masako's way of admitting that her true feelings lay in that direction. Yet she felt she still had an obligation to Kōzō and the life they had shared for nearly five years. Under the circumstances she was surprised that she felt any obligation at all to Kōzō. Perhaps for the moment she merely wanted tranquility more than anything else. But this only lasted through the month of August.

The beginning of the new school term was approaching, and Kōzō set out for Tokyo day after day saying he had to use the library. And, of course he occasionally spent the night in Tokyo. One morning as he was putting on his shoes in the entry hall, he said, "Well, after all is said and done, things have turned out quite well. You realize by now that you can't leave me; for one thing, you have no place to go. You can't live on family pride, you know, not these days." He finished tying his shoes and stood facing Masako. "I expect I'll go on having these little flings with other women. And no doubt you'll get jealous as you did the last time, but you really have no place to go. Once you realize that, you'll just be sensible and close your eyes to these things. That's the smart thing to do. After all, these other women are just prostitutes, but you're well respected as the wife of a university professor."

"That's right," replied Masako blandly. She gazed blankly at her husband and wondered if he really believed she still loved him after what had happened. She remembered the ridiculous spectacle he had made of himself at Tsukiji, and looking at him now she realized it could not have been any other way. After she had called him a pretentious bastard he had been very blunt with her and did not try to hide anything. It was not very pleasant for her to contemplate what her life would be like to go on as his wife and to have to put up with such a man day and night. It was asking too much. She knew he was not stupid, but that he had just confused willfulness with dignity. Occasionally when students came to visit, he would shamelessly praise his own books. Masako could not stand the sight of such a man.

The days passed in succession, and Masako felt like this more and more often. She also thought about her cousin. Indeed, she had thought of him often since that sunny August day when she had returned from Inamuragasaki, and she made up her mind to visit him again. It seemed that in all her life no one had ever loved her as much as Shuntarō.

One Wednesday morning early in September, Masako saw her husband off to work and then took a kimono to a dyer in Yuigahama to have it recolored. She stopped at the Genjidō on her way home. To her surprise there were no masks on the shelf. The shopkeeper's wife noticed Masako looking at the shelf and said, "We've been having a problem with Mr. Mibu. He says he is tired of carving masks. My husband has urged him several times to make more, but he won't do it. There is a growing interest in the Nō theatre these days and the masks were just beginning to really sell. He's a strange one."

According to the shopkeeper, up until this spring they had taken the masks on consignment and had sold them for five thousand yen each. The shop kept thirty percent and Shuntarō got the rest. Recently, they had been buying the masks from him for three thousand yen each. They generally sold about seven masks a month, and they also received orders from department stores in Tokyo. The woman could just not understand why Shuntarō had given up such a lucrative enterprise.

"The last time I stopped here was in early July. There were three masks on display then."

"After we sold those, he didn't bring anymore. Apparently he hasn't carved any since spring. The ones you saw here then had all been carved earlier. Recently a leading Nō actor even came to see the masks. He had seen one a friend had bought here. He thought it was very good and asked to see some more. Mr. Mibu says he won't carve any more masks, but the funny thing about it is that he is carving trays, brooches, mirror stands—the kind of things we could never get him to carve before."

Masaaki TACHIHARA

It was painfully clear to Masako that all the things he had told her that day were true. Perhaps the chance encounter with his mother after an interval of sixteen years had affected him more than Masako had realized. Still, she felt this abrupt change was just a little too sudden. She had the feeling that he had been walking a straight line and had suddenly been sidetracked.

In the shop was a poster, just like last year, announcing that this year's Takiginō would be held on September thirtieth. Masako knew that since her marriage it had been her custom to reckon the passing of the years by the succession of posters announcing the Takiginō. In her memory she retained a vivid image of the Kofukuji Temple in Nara and of the bright torches of the Takiginō carving their pattern on the darkness of the night.

Even after she left the Genjidō, Masako could see in her mind the fires of the Takiginō. In the spring of the year when she was eighteen, Masako had not been aware of the full significance of the torchlight Nō. But that year had been significant for Masako in two ways. Up until then she and Shuntarō had sometimes slept in the same bed. She had played the role of both sister and mother for him. Before they set out on that trip to Nara, they had been aware of their close blood relationship. Although they never went beyond certain limits, they had been able to create their own happy world. Then when she saw Shuntarō against the background of the flaming torches, she became conscious of something emblematic of eternity. Perhaps it was because she, too, had the same background. Or perhaps it was because the image of Shuntarō superimposed on the eternal patterns of the Nō filled her mind. Once before their trip to Nara they had slept together, and he had touched her breasts. He must have been unconsciously seeking his mother. Now as Masako admitted her true feelings for Shuntarō, those very feelings seemed like a cruel punishment she had to suffer.

Masako did not know what to do. She had nothing to do at home. If she spent too much time there alone, she would find herself thinking about Shuntarō. She stopped walking and stood for awhile looking at the white, sandy ground beneath her feet. She felt that their close blood relationship was now irrelevant. She considered the fact that she had been both sister and mother to Shuntarō and decided that their close blood relationship no longer mattered. Their present situation seemed like a kind of punishment for her request that he not marry until she had borne a child. 'Since he gave up carving masks, I'm all he has left,' she thought. It seemed that the only thing that remained for either of them was to love each other.

By now Masako found herself standing in front of her own house. She turned around and set out for Inamuragasaki.

10

Shuntarō was carving a tray. He did not turn around or give any sign that he noticed when Masako arrived.

He kept his broad back to her and went on working with his chisel.

She entered the room, "Shuntarō, I came to visit you again."

He made no reply; only his hands and chisel kept moving.

"Why don't you turn around?"

"I thought I told you not to come here again."

"That's right—I was at the Genjidō today. The woman there was complaining that you aren't carving masks anymore."

"What good are those masks? To go on doing that is just a waste of time."

"That's not so. Why do you say things like that?"

"As far as I'm concerned, I only carved the masks to make money. You could say I had to do it. A Nō mask should be made so that it can reflect every changing emotion, but I could only make each mask express one emotion. When that one emotion was destroyed for me, carving masks no longer had any meaning. The last time you were here, I was still feeling sad that I wasn't carving masks anymore."

"You're trying to justify what you did by saying you had to do it. Isn't it enough that you simply did it? Please don't talk about it anymore."

"Up to now, whenever I made a mask, I was always trying to recreate my mother's face. I made all kinds of masks—Zōonna, Magojirō, and Fushikizō, but in that one respect they were all the same."

"I knew that."

"You did?" For the first time since she had arrived, he

put down the chisel and turned to face her.

"I've known that for a long time."

"Even though I've always thought of my mother as I carved those masks, in another sense, all of them are your face too. Did you know that?"

"I've known that for a long time, too. I knew it, but it seemed there was nothing I could do about it. I think you've been in the same position. Doesn't it come from the fact that we've always felt that being cousins is a barrier between us?"

"No one is to blame. I've always been aware of how sad you've been since you got married. But what could I do about it? I feel now that I have lived far too constricted a life. There must have been a better way to live."

"You have regrets for the past?"

"No. I have never had any regrets about the past. To tell the truth, I found that my life was nearly unbearable after you left. Twice I considered killing myself. Both times I decided for the most trivial reasons to go on living. From the outside my life probably seemed very straightforward and simple the way I devoted myself to soccer and to carving medieval Nō masks. But I never believed in soccer as a cure. The most I can say for it is that when I really got involved in it, I forgot about everything else. And as for carving those masks, even I sometimes thought it a sorry way to spend my life. I could only believe in it when I was carving what I wanted to carve. I was lying when I said I thought there was something of eternal value in doing that. Oh, sometimes I really believed that Nō masks were the real thing and would live on while the things of the modern world

175

would soon pass away. I wonder if you ever felt that you could see something eternal in me, Masako? I know I've sensed it in you. But even if we have both felt this, it was all in our minds, just a figment of our imaginations. Our family has fallen apart and we were only thinking of these things as a way of escaping reality. That kind of eternal value never really existed."

He stood up and came to Masako, "Why did you come here? Did you hope to find something eternal?" He put his arms around Masako's shoulders and pulled her to him. She looked into his bloodshot eyes and felt his hot breath on her face.

"Shuntarō, what are you doing?"

"I warned you about coming back here."

Masako closed her eyes; she felt her *obi* being loosened. She made no effort to resist. Her decision to come here today had been made on the spur of the moment, but all along she had known intuitively what he had meant when he warned her not to come back.

The room was brightly lit and Masako kept her eyes closed and murmured softly, "This is the first time I have ever been unfaithful to my husband." And yet today she knew that in all the years she had been married to Kōzō, she had been waiting for this day. In the middle of the sundrenched room their two bodies twined together.

"What wonderful breasts! I remember I touched them once a long time ago."

Masako felt the warm thrill of his hands on her breasts.

The sun moved and the room was filled with light. It

was evening when Masako at last became aware of the pounding of the distant ocean.

11

When Masako left the Nō pavilion she believed fully that a transformation had taken place within her. Walking down the mountain path she was determined now to leave her husband.

But no sooner had she arrived home than her husband came home, and seeing his cheerful face she was overcome with guilt at what she had done that afternoon. She reverted to the role of good housewife and that night attended her husband with unusual tenderness. After Kōzō had gone to sleep, she lay awake wondering if the warm tingle of her skin was any different from the sensation she had experienced that afternoon. It was a difficult night for her, but she could hardly bear to face the light of dawn when it came.

Kōzō did not go anywhere that day but remained shut away in his study. In the afternoon Masako left the house saying she had shopping to do. She went straight to Inamuragasaki. She had lost her self-confidence and the resolve she had felt the day before.

She tried to rekindle the passionate warmth she had experienced the day before, but she no longer believed that a transformation had occurred. She no longer fully understood her feelings for Shuntarō. As she walked down the mountain path later, she felt far more regret than she had the night before.

For a week after that, she restrained herself and stayed home attending to her husband's needs. The obvious thing to do was to leave her husband whom she did not love, and go to her cousin whom she did love, and yet she lacked the self-confidence to do this. The relationship with her cousin was not clear enough.

12

The day for the performance of the Takiginō was nearly at hand. As the time approached when the torches of the Takiginō would carve flaming patterns on the darkness of the night, a vision of the coming fire became clearer in Masako's mind. Now that her relationship with Shuntarō had changed, her vision of the fires took on a wholly different meaning.

On the morning of September eighteenth shortly after her husband had left for work, Masako received a letter from her cousin. It was delivered by an old woman. No doubt he had the letter delivered personally to make certain that Kōzō did not see it.

Masako, don't come here again. Both of us have only been chasing dreams, we're being unrealistic. I will always consider the intimacy I've shared with you as one of my greatest joys, so why is it that when we two are together I can feel nothing but a sense of doom?

In the past I've known a number of women; they meant no more to me than playing soccer. But with you it is different, it won't work. Even when I am with you I can only feel a sense of futility. The truth is we've been able to support each other because of our similar circumstances, but we can't go on like this. Your father was killed in the war, my father was killed by an American soldier. Grandfather walked with them once through the streets of Nara, and later he walked there again with us, his grandchildren. Do you remember what he said to us that day? He said that we two could find something of eternal value in each other. This discovery would not be something we could convey to anyone else. I wonder if we have really found and shared that something of eternal value?

Do you remember when our parents were still alive, when we used to play "show each other?" The day I found out you were going to be married, I thought back nostalgically to those days. Barely five years have passed since then, but to me the time seems much longer. The other day I knew how mature your body had become and I realized that we could never go back to the days when we were children. The very fullness of your body saddened me. I was sad that we have soiled our lives, sad that we can no longer return to the pure days of our childhood; that was the kind of sadness I felt. And in this sadness I felt that gathering sense of doom.

When I think of what the future holds for us, it seems that the torches of the Takiginō we saw in Nara are not the flames of eternity, but rather the fire of destruction. In the past we have often talked about those torches and what they mean. I tell you, Masako, they signify destruction. I myself do not know what it means that I see the torches of the sacred ritual of the Takiginō as the fire of destruction. The other day, Masako, as I held your rich body in my arms it seemed as though I could see those torches flickering and burning in the darkness. If I go on living, I will always feel this way.

Why is it I can only think in terms of destruction? Masako, if you know the answer, please tell me.

So, we must not meet again. Perhaps I will get married soon, or if not, perhaps I will find a woman to live with me. The woman I told you about, the one at the market, has fortunately abandoned me in favor of a wealthy patron. I will find a younger woman this time. Up to now I've always lived my life refusing to recognize despair. Now I have decided to live by seeking a glimmer of hope. And so, goodbye.

P.S. In a few days I will deliver a Magojirō mask at the Genjidō. It is for you, please pick it up there. It is the last mask I will ever carve. Grandfather once told me that the original of the Magojirō masks we have today was a mask carved by a Nō actor named Magojirō who was the fourth generation of the Kongō School of Nō. He carved the mask in the image of his beautiful, dead wife. It pleases me to follow this old tradition.

The realization that she and Shuntarō were both alone swirled and grew in Masako's mind. The sense of destruction he had seen in the torches corresponded to something Masako had found within herself. The sense of destruction seen in the fire of the sacred Nō ritual had nothing to do with the usual Nō performance. It seemed that when the torches were extinguished at the end of the play, the fortunes of the venerable old Mibu family would also come to an end. Although there was beauty to be seen in the eternal patterns of the Nō, that beauty was not of this modern world. In the torchlight of the Takiginō which they had seen in Nara years ago, these two, without realizing it, had seen their own end. For both of them the red flames were emblematic of their destiny — a destiny they shared in the deaths of their fathers and the separation from their mothers. Both had always lived with this vision of the fire.

When she married Kōzō, Masako had a dream, a dream of loving her husband, of having children, of raising them — but in the course of five years the dream had dissipated. Apart from her responsibility as a wife, it seemed that her life with Kōzō was without meaning.

What was this glimmer of hope Shuntarō had spoken of, for which he would live? Had there ever been any hope?

Perhaps as they walked through the streets of Nara, their grandfather, Tokinobu, had kindled the possibility of hope in the hearts of his two grandchildren even as he himself was walking the path of destruction. Masako could still remember clearly how her grandfather had looked at that time. She had gone every year to see the

Takiginō, but she had not gone to see the play; rather, she had been attracted by the consuming pattern of fire-light against the dark night. She understood this now. And now that she had come to know her cousin, she felt that nothing was visible to her but those flames.

Masako felt that all her life she had been looking up at the blue sky. But now, in the corners and around the edges of the emptiness she could see the flicker of red flames.

Day after day as she watched these flames dancing in the emptiness around her, Masako began to see them superimposed on the flaming candles that surrounded the altar at her grandfather's funeral. And forming yet another layer of flickering fire beyond, was the waver-ing light of her father's and her uncle's funeral candles. At such moments it seemed that death had taken every-thing from her and all that remained was her cousin. She wondered sometimes why she went on living and could see very clearly the position she was in that made that question inevitable.

Masako loved her father who had died during the war and her mother who had left her, she loved her grand-father who was dead, she had loved her uncle who was dead, and she loved Shuntarō. Each of these loves had been accompanied by an unbearable weight of sadness. 'Must Shuntarō and I go on living after all the others have been taken from us—destroyed?' These two who knew such love and who knew this sadness of having been left behind would be destroyed by the very vio-lence of their existence.

One day Masako stood on the veranda and watched

182

the gathering twilight. She could see the flames licking around the edges of the void. Layer upon layer of wavering flames were superimposed on one another. Another day just at noon as she stood in the garden which was bathed in autumn sunlight, she looked up into the emptiness and knew in the depths of her being the beauty of death. With it came a feeling of relief she had never before experienced.

The following day Masako began to buy and to accumulate small quantities of sleeping pills. Now the only thing that remained was to find out whether or not Shuntarō felt as she did.

13

On the morning of September thirtieth, the day the Takiginō was to be held, Masako saw her husband off as usual. A short while later she left the house carrying a bundle that contained a letter addressed to her mother and the Magojirō mask she had picked up at the Genjidō.

Her cousin was not there when she arrived at the Nō pavilion in Inamuragasaki. She wondered if he was out seeing the woman at the market.

Masako entered the pavilion and began sweeping and cleaning the stage and its connecting bridge. Next she swept out the greenroom that her cousin had been using for a work room. She carefully stacked the carvings he was still working on. It was eleven o'clock by the time she had finished cleaning.

Feeling it would be some time before her cousin returned, she took out the letter she had written to her mother the previous day and read it over.

Since you now belong to another family, I am sorry to have to ask a favor of you, but please remember this is the only favor I have asked of you as a daughter.

Shuntarō once told me that he had no hard feelings at all for his own mother and that he found a great deal of satisfaction in achieving this state of mind. I want you to know that I feel the same way about you.

For the past seventeen years Shuntarō and I have always gotten along by supporting each other. We have always tried to be brave and not to complain. Grandfather died just two months after you attended my wedding. By that time the old family house had already passed into other hands and only the Nō pavilion remained. Since my marriage, Shuntarō has been living alone in the Nō pavilion. I have always been both mother and sister to him.

I don't know why things turned out this way, but it has reached the point where neither of us can bear to go on living. It is not that my life with Kōzō has been unhappy; I feel that he has been an excellent husband. And yet, I do not feel that I can ask this favor of him. When you receive this letter, please come to the Nō pavilion at the old house.

Grandfather gave me some money as a wedding present. I never spent it and it is now deposited in my bank in Kamakura. Please use it to take care of any expenses. My official seal is also at the bank and with it you will have access to my account. If there is any money left over, I would be pleased if you will spend it on my brother and sister whom I have never had a chance to meet.

Masako

This letter had been written with a brush on a long roll of paper. Masako had been taught to use a writing brush by her grandfather, but this was the first time she had used it since her marriage. Masako recalled how serene her feelings had been the day before as she wrote these words.

Shuntarō returned shortly after noon.

"I knew you'd come back." His breath smelled of alcohol and his eyes were bloodshot.

"Isn't it a little early to be drinking?"

"I haven't had anything yet today; this is just the result of last night's drinking. You know the woman at the market I wrote to you about in that letter? Well, I've been sleeping with her some nights when her patron doesn't show up."

"I don't care to hear about it. Thank you for the Magojirō mask, I brought it with me today."

"Don't you want it?"

"Of course I want it. I came today because I have something very important to talk to you about. I hope you will listen."

"Masako, you know I will listen to anything you have to say."

"All right. After you hear what I have to say, if you don't want to do it, please say so clearly."

"What do you want me to do?"

"In the letter you sent the other day you said you could go on living because you could see a faint glimmer of hope. So—tell me Shuntarō, what is there to hope for, really?"

"Right now there's nothing. I meant I'd find it someday."

"You think you'll find it someday—If I told you that I have nothing to hope for in the future, would you try to give me something to hope for?"

"Masako, we really don't have anything to hope for as long as both of us feel we cannot be lovers because we are cousins." Shuntarō's eyes glowed for a moment.

"You're right. Why don't you read this instead of listening to me talk." Masako placed before him the letter she had written to her mother. Shuntarō picked up the envelope, looked at it front and back, and put it down.

"Aren't you going to read it?"

"Is it your will?"

Masako said nothing, but held his gaze with her own. After a moment Shuntarō took the letter from the envelope and after reading the first few lines, put it back.

"Aren't you going to read it?"

"I think I know what it says without reading the whole thing." He looked around and noticed that the room had been freshly cleaned. "Today is the day of the Takiginō."

"Ever since I read your letter I have been seeing the

fire of those torches burning in the darkness."

"Is everything finished between you and Mr. Izumi?"

"I think this would have happened even if I had never known Kōzō. Perhaps it's just that the blood we inherited from the Mibu family was not meant to survive in the modern world."

Both sat for a time in silence. The letter lay between them. Both dropped their eyes and stared at the name written on the front of the envelope.

"We might as well do it." Shuntarō spoke simply, but the expression on his face was tense.

"Shuntarō—"

"I won't complain. I've never acted irresponsibly up to now, Masako, so don't worry about this. I'm happy. You read what I wrote in that letter, but the truth is I could not imagine living without you. It's not surprising that we both just happened to have the same thought. They say the path of life has all sorts of strange turnings; this is one of them. Masako, let me hold you in my arms once more."

"Yes," said Masako reddening. "I'm yours. It's been this way from the first, you're the only man I've ever loved."

Shuntarō explained that the mail was picked up at the nearby post box at three o'clock. If they mailed the letter after that, it would be picked up the next morning and delivered at the home of Masako's mother a day later.

At four o'clock Shuntarō went out to mail the letter. Then they went for a walk in the nearby hills through the fallen autumn leaves. They agreed they would depart from this world in surroundings that had been familiar to them since childhood. Afterwards they returned to the Nō pavilion and took pleasure in making love for the final time. They were surrounded by silence. Outside the autumn sunset adorned the sky.

They moved their bedding to the Nō stage and placed their pillows side by side—Shuntarō's on the left, Masako's on the right. Their beds faced the back of the stage.

Both felt their emotions calmed by thoughts of their grandfather and of the many others who had danced on this stage.

They returned to the other room and divided the sleeping pills. Neither of them knew how many were needed to make a lethal dose, and they did not know if they had enough to kill themselves or not. Masako had read somewhere that taking too many of these pills produced the opposite effect and would not be lethal.

"Somehow you look as though you are happy."

"I am, Masako, I feel I have lived a full life. I was just remembering how we used to play 'show each other.'" Even as he spoke these words a pained expression passed across Shuntarō's face.

At Shuntarō's request they made love yet again—they did it again and again. Never before had they made love with such power and intensity. After sating themselves, they went to the Nō stage and lay down.

"Listen! Do you hear the sound of Nō music?"

"Yes. This is our own personal Takiginō, performed just for the two of us."

Still dressed in her pale blue kimono, Masako removed only her *obi* when she lay down. Shuntarō changed into a dark blue kimono that had belonged to his grandfather. They each bound their ankles and knees.

The slanting rays of the setting sun penetrated the Nō pavilion, and the well-polished wooden pillars and boards glowed with a brilliant lustre. Soon the glow of sunlight had reached their feet and everything around ·them was stained a fiery red. Masako put on her Mago- jirō mask, the last one Shuntarō had carved. He put on a Chūjō* mask that had belonged to their grandfather.

Having completed all their preparations, they clasped each other's hands. "It's just like when we were children," said Shuntarō.

"You're right. Everything else has changed, we alone are unchanged."

Through the Nō masks they could see the sun setting. By now the Kamakura Takiginō would be beginning.

"Masako?"

"Yes?"

"Can you see the flames, like the ones we saw that time in Nara?"

"I see them, yes."

"We'll be meeting grandfather again soon. I don't re- member my father's face very clearly, but we'll soon see him again too."

"Yes, of course. Shuntarō, is there anything else we need to say to each other?"

"No – Well, if I said I still want to live awhile longer, would it sound like I had some misgivings?"

"Shuntarō! If you really feel that way, we can still get help for you. You can be saved." Masako remembered the pained expression on her cousin's face as he took the sleeping pills.

"That's not what I meant. It just feels like I am leaving

something unfinished. I guess the truth is that the only things I'm leaving behind are debts."

"I mentioned that in the letter I sent to my mother. I asked that any debts be paid with the money left in my bank account."

"That was thoughtful of you. This way I can die happily and no one will think badly of me when I'm gone. I've never been unhappy, you know."

"I'm glad."

After that they were silent. The sun set and darkness descended on the stage.

Masako was not sure how much time passed after that; she felt very, very sleepy. She called out her cousin's name, but there was no response. She tried shaking his hands, but there was no feeling even in her own. At that moment Masako heard the hard, piercing sound of the Nō flute. Soon the large drum joined in. She could hear the clear voices of the chorus. The music seemed to come from the sides of the stage where the orchestra and chorus sit during a performance. Soon the shoulder drum joined the music. A Nō dancer appeared on the stage, but Masako could not tell which dance he was performing.

Just as the throbbing beat of the drum grew most intense, it seemed to Masako that she could see the flaming torches of the Takiginō coming down on them from above. There appeared layer upon layer of flaming torches and beyond them she could make out her grandfather's face, her father's face, her uncle's face. "Shuntarō!" she tried to cry out, but no sound came. Still, one part of her mind remained conscious. It seemed to her suddenly that she had been unreasonable in luring Shuntarō to his death. All she could do now was pray that neither of them survived. It would be impossible for one of them to go on living without the other.

GLOSSARY

p. 21   *"kendo"*   The traditional Japanese martial art of swordsmanship.

p. 26   "Meiji period"   1868-1912

p. 91   "Heian period"   794-1185

         "Kamakura period"   1185-1333

         "Momoyama period"   1568-1600

         "Shigetō bow"   The traditional wicker bow used in the art of Yabusame.

p. 99   "Yayoi no Sato"   Yayoi is the old name for March, the month associated traditionally with young girls. Sato means a small village.

p. 130   The masks play an important part in this story. All are drawn from the ancient Japanese drama, the Nō. Each mask has specific meaning for the Nō actor and his audience.

         "Zōonna"   The mask of a young, graceful woman exuding propriety, correctness, and formality. It is associated with the cherry blossom deity.

         "Fushikizō"   The youthfulness of this mask contrasts with the decorum of the Zōonna. It suggests a woman who has rejected the banalities of humanity and embraced the peacefulness of nature.

         "Magojirō"   This mask represents a gentle, young wife and is the standard one for the roles of young women.

p. 142   *"sushi"*   A unique Japanese dish consisting of vinegared rice and usually raw, salt water fish, served with soy sauce and green horseradish.

p. 143   "Deigan"   This mask is used mainly for women sworn to exact revenge as spirits, or for dead women suffering torments in hell.

         "Koomote"   The mask of a young girl suffused with youthful beauty.

p. 189   "Chujō"   Shuntarō's mask is that of ideal and youthful nobility of spirit.